LISSY-LOST!

Written and Illustrated by
Lori Taylor

Bear Track Press
Pinckney, MI

Second Edition

ISBN: 1-59286-964-5
Published by BEAR TRACK PRESS
A subsidiary of BEAR TRACK STUDIOS, LLC
www.beartrackstudiosllc.com
www.loritaylorart.com
Pinckney, MI

Printed in the United States of America

For
"Elizabeth"

"All who wander are not lost."
– J. R. R. Tolkien

Also by Lori Taylor:

Crazy Cat Don't Chase That Rabbit
(Wild Trail Tales Graphic Reader)
Hot Times in the Big Creek Wood
(Wild Trail Tales Graphic Reader)

Holly Wild: Bamboozled on Beaver Island (Book 1)
Holly Wild: Let Sleeping Bear Dunes Lie (Book 2)
Holly Wild: Packing for the Porkies (Book 3)
Holly Wild: Questpedition for da
Yooper Stone! (Book 4)
Holly Wild: The Young GeEK's Guide to
Getting Outside! (Picture Book)
Holly Wild: Sketch-n-Color Book (Coloring Book)

www.loritaylorart.com
www.beartrackpress.com

Thank you
to my family of friends

CHAPTER ONE – Lissy's Wish

The crisp evening air, promising snow, bit at Lissy's nose. She listened to the trees around her dropping the last of their leaves. Indian Summer would be over all too soon and Thanksgiving would arrive. A chilling breeze caught the last few leafy stragglers.

Just like me, Lissy thought, pulling on her red mittens, *always last, and too chicken to jump.* The golden leaves swirled about her and she watched them fall to the ground. "Catch one from the treetop, and you'll get your wish," Grandma Brown once told her.

The thought of her grandmother suddenly made Lissy sad. Three weeks had passed since she had died and Lissy was still feeling the pain and loneliness from her loss. She was holding the ragged, handmade book of a Child's Garden of Verses, and she hugged it tighter. The book was a comforting thing because it reminded Lissy of her beloved grandmother. When she was born, a woman that her grandmother knew had made the book for Lissy. The woman had cut each delicate letter and picture out of magazines and glued them onto bright yellow cloth. Whenever her grandmother visited, they would take the book out and sit for hours, looking at the pictures and reading the musical rhymes. Grandma had always said that there were secrets hidden in these pictures and rhymes, meant only for Lissy—that's why it was special. Its worn, soft cover felt like her grandmother's cotton summer dress and smelled of her rose water perfume, and so had become even more special. It was the one thing in Lissy's life that gave color to days of gray. She gave the book one more hug and placed it on the table for her mother to pack into the car.

Lissy, her brother, Bob, and their parents had spent the weekend at her uncle's cabin up in the northern woods. She had always loved the music of the lake and pines and often felt that it was her real home. Now they were closing up the cabin and packing the car to go home. Lissy inhaled the spicy sweetness of leaf litter and decided to run down the wooden steps to say goodbye to the lake.

Her moment of autumn bliss was shattered by the sound of Bob running down the steps behind her. She hurried down the last few, in hopes that he wouldn't push her down them again.

"Out of the way, Geek," he yelled, his blonde hair flying as he passed her.

Bob was four years older than Lissy and at thirteen, was already changing into a young man. He was smart, athletic, and handsome. She would never be like Bob, and her own mother often reminded her of that. But even though he was sometimes mean to her, she couldn't help but to be in awe of him. She secretly wished she could be like him and win the love of her parents. Instead, she was clumsy, awkward, and dumb, and she was sure that would never change.

Bob ran to the end of the dock to throw stones out into the shallow, sandy lake. The wind blew across the gray water, making silvery-white foam that frosted the waves.

"Mother said to watch out for the white cats!" she yelled to Bob, trying to spoil his fun. "They'll take you away and drown you!"

"You mean the white caps, *stupid.* They only get you if you're swimming. Gosh, how can you be so *dumb?"* he said to her as he skipped a stone across the choppy water. The setting sun slipped behind a bank of angry-looking clouds nearly the same color as the water. An icy gust blew across the lake and lifted Lissy's collar, slapping her in the face. She looked away so that Bob couldn't see the tears in her eyes. That was just one more thing he could tease her about—being a crybaby.

I wish I could be here always. I don't want to go back home, she thought as her wet, blue eyes followed the last golden leaf from the top of the maple nearest the shore.

It twirled and spun, gracefully floating downward. Lissy reached out and it landed in her hand.

"It fits like a glove," she said, pressing it close to her chest as if to lock this beautiful lake memory inside her heart. Holding it out before her, she let the wind take her wish. She watched the leaf as it caught the breeze and sailed across the lake.

She looked up at Bob, who was still skipping stones. Then she heard Mother call for them in the distance. *Her wish didn't come true, they were ready to leave.* Another hot tear escaped and slid down her icy cheek.

CHAPTER TWO – The Gift

Lissy walked down to the water's edge to say goodbye to the darting minnows and the little crayfish that swam backwards. For an instant, sunlight peeked through the racing clouds and sparkled bright upon the water.

That's when she saw it. Lissy caught a glimpse of something red bobbing up and down near the dock. There, tangled in the weeds, was a small plastic canoe, not much longer than her finger. Her heart leaped at the prize before her! She took off her mitten and pulled the canoe out of the water. She smiled, turning it over in her hand. It was perfectly detailed. She ran her finger over the smooth toy and noticed a small chunk taken out of its left side. What a wonderful surprise, this little gift from the lake!

Suddenly remembering Bob, she looked up quickly to see if he was watching. Lissy jammed the canoe into her deep coat pocket, just as Bob turned around, eyeing her as if she were up to something. Lissy stood up, kicked a stone into the water and ran to the steps.

"Lissy! Bob! Let's *go*, it'll be dark soon," Mother called, her eyes flashing the same gray-green as her silk skirt and jacket. She wore strings of pearls and pearl cluster earrings. Even the silver hat set upon her head like a crown had pearls fixed into its white netting, glistening like water droplets. She looked like a queen, standing tall and regal, her long silver-streaked dark blonde hair bound up and pinned tightly into a bun.

Lissy started up the steps and tripped on her brown coat. It was a hand-me-down from one of her aunts and was three times too large, but her mother said she would grow into it.

Bob sprinted up the steps behind her and knocked her down. "Race ya, Geek," he laughed cruelly.

Lissy ignored his mean nickname for her and wiped her hands on her coat. She reached into her pocket to make sure her little red boat was still there and moved her mitten over it to keep it snug and secure. By the time she reached the top of the steps, snowflakes had started falling quietly through the air.

"Look, it's snowing!" she announced as her parents finished packing the car.

"Settle down, Lissy, we have a long trip home," Mother said in her usual tone of command. She hustled Lissy through the open car door and slammed it shut.

Bob stuck his tongue out at Lissy and delved into one of his dumb old books about cowboys. He was always reading. He was the smart one, as Mother and Father often told her.

"Why can't you be like your brother?" they asked.

Those were the times she especially wanted to run away and be with her Grandma Brown. She never, ever laughed at Lissy or called her dumb.

But now she was gone, the only one who ever showed kindness to Lissy, except for her Uncle Ward. He was rich and bought them ice cream. He owned an umbrella company and could afford to do that, Mother had said. He often gave her scraps of colored silk and taffeta, and last Christmas he had given Lissy her most favorite doll in the world. She had long, black hair and crystal blue eyes, not at all like Lissy with her dull, silver-blue eyes and mousy, brown hair her mother kept in a plain pageboy cut. When she saw the beautiful doll in her blue satin gown, she named her Los Angelees. She had heard the name in school, and thought it sounded so elegant and sophisticated, just like her new doll. Her parents laughed and Bob teased her saying, "That's the name of a city, you idiot." But that made her love the name all the more. Los Angelees became her secret magic name and she only used it when she was alone so that no one would make fun of her.

After her grandmother had died, she kept the doll and her book close to her, rarely putting either down. Lissy had quiet tea parties and whispered poems and verses to Los Angelees from her "good book," the name she gave her cloth book. But her mother reprimanded her, saying that there is only one "Good Book" and that certainly was not it. She said that Lissy was too old to play with such baby things. She should be reading real books and concentrating on her schoolwork, like Bob. But Lissy read the words of her book over and over. She thought that if she memorized them, someday something magical would happen.

The car started down the long, winding road. Lissy tossed her brown hair from side to side, looking for all of her things. Bob had hidden Los Angelees under a blanket between them.

"Mother, Bob hid my doll trying to scare me!"

He looked sideways at her and snickered.

"Hush, Lissy, and sit still, can't you see that your father is driving!" her mother hissed at her like an angry cat.

She hated it when her mother talked to her like that. "My real name is Elizabeth," she whispered quietly, "like the queen."

Bob heard this and laughed, "No it's not, it's Geek." He turned toward the window, straining to see the words better in the dying light, and brought his book closer to his face to read.

Lissy looked under the blanket for her book. Not finding it, she got down on her knees and crawled on the floor, looking under things. After frantically searching her side of the car, she sat up with a lump in her throat. On the verge of panic and choking back tears, she said, "Bob, did you take my book?"

"I don't take your stupid book. You left it on the table

8

in the cabin, *stupid,"* he snorted.

"Mother, did you pack my book?" Lissy asked with a slight feeling of hope.

"Lissy, you know very well that I told you to have everything packed into the car and to be ready to go. You'll just have to wait until next year to get it," her mother said. Her gray-green eyes were as cold as the waters that held the white cats, waiting to claw at her.

"NO! Turn around, now! We have to go back and get it!" Lissy scrambled around in her seat, looking back at the snow-covered road. The sky shone an angry red as the sun disappeared behind the rows of trees.

"Lissy, sit still," her father spoke sternly.

"Big *baby,"* Bob mumbled, pulling the blanket over him to nap.

She couldn't breathe—panic set upon her chest like a brick. She felt like a prisoner, even more so than the time Bob's friends tied her to huge sunflowers that towered over her, grinning like old hags. She pulled her collar tightly around her, sobbing silently. The "good book" was the only way she could keep bad things from happening to her. It had the magical words in it. It held the memory of Grandma, of her soft cheeks, musical laugh, and rosy perfume, and of her holding Lissy on her lap reading to her. Lissy suddenly felt both angry and terrified, like a wounded animal that everyone enjoyed torturing.

The car bumped along. With tears streaming down her face, Lissy kneeled on the seat, looking through the rear windshield down the road that led back to her most precious possession, her "good book."

She pulled at her hair and desperately tried to remember the pictures and poems, to recall their magical words.

That's when her father hit a large pothole in the road, and everything changed *forever*.

CHAPTER THREE –
The Adventure Begins

The car door flung open so quickly that Lissy was stunned at first. The sudden blast of cold air took her breath away, and then she was weightless for an instant as she fell soundlessly out of the car. Her feeling of flight ended in a hurry as she landed with a hard thump in the middle of the snow-covered gravel road.

Her mouth still open in disbelief, she watched the door slam back into place as the large, black car chugged through the curtain of snow and over the hill. She heard it backfire once in the distance, as if adding a final insult that said, "good riddance."

Everything was quiet now, as Lissy sat and watched the giant flakes drop around her in the evening air. She thought, for a moment, that it was very pretty and felt that she had never been so free or at peace. But soon that feeling was replaced by aches in every part of her body from the jolt of the fall from the car.

"Mother?" she called weakly. Her voice sounded tiny. The word just floated past her like a papery moth and disappeared into the forest. She stood up, brushing the snow from her coat and rubbed her sore bottom. She didn't feel too much like a queen now. She looked for her mittens, but found only the one stuffed in her pocket. She started to cry. It began to snow harder, and Lissy walked around in circles, dazed and stiff-legged like a wind-up toy soldier. Now she was in big trouble. She didn't know what to do or where to go, so Lissy just stood there in the middle of the road and cried.

"I'm sorry, I'm sorry!" she sobbed. The tears gushed from her eyes, making it hard to see. Everything was so unfair, everyone was so mean, and she was so young to have all of this happen to her. The once friendly trees now seemed to tower over her like giant, twisted black beasts, their arms outstretched to grab her. She cried harder and began shaking. Lissy was cold, frightened, and utterly alone.

Suddenly, she felt a great blanket of calm fall over her and she stopped crying. A tiny chickadee hopped about on the road in the last rays of light, chattering at

Lissy. Out of nowhere, Lissy heard herself reciting one of the poems from her "good book":

> *"I know that 'til tomorrow*
> *I shall see the sun arise,*
> *No ugly dream shall fright my mind,*
> *No ugly sight my eyes.*
> *And now at last,*
> *The sun is going down behind the wood,*
> *And I am very happy*
> *For I know that I've been good."*

Lissy smiled. She was proud of herself for remembering the words.

The little bird hopped to the side of the road and paused, then flew up onto a pine branch and looked at her. She didn't know what else to do so she followed it in the grayness. Its tiny, white belly glowed like a small lantern and it led Lissy deeper into the forest, stopping occasionally to wait for her to catch up.

It had become very dark now and Lissy found herself under a thick canopy of pines when the chickadee finally settled on a tree. Lissy sat down upon the soft carpet of needles and pulled her coat collar up high around her head. She was now thankful that her coat was three times too large, as it had become her tent.

Among the trees, the forest night was cold and quiet. The little bird roosted on the branch above her, tucking its black head into its fluffy feathers to stay warm. Everything had happened so fast, and she still didn't know what she was going to do. Her body ached badly from the fall, but Lissy felt safe here and very sleepy, and she soon drifted off.

For a moment, the snow stopped and the moon shone brightly, lighting the forest like a lamp. A little light filtered down upon Lissy, waking her from her sleep, and she looked up. Although the branches obscured most of the moon, she could just barely make out the face of the little girl singing there. At home, when Lissy would wake up afraid in the middle of the night, that little girl singing her silent moon song had always made Lissy feel better.

But while the light of the moon was comforting, it also cast gray-purple shadows across the snow here and there, like nets waiting to snare her. She heard small snapping and crackling sounds all around her and thought, *It's probably the Bogeymen that Bob always teased me about, crunching bones of little girls lost in the woods.* She hid her face in her coat and sang to herself.

"Farewell, 'O brother, sister, sire!
'O pleasant party round the fire!
The songs you sing, the tales you tell,
'Til far to-morrow fare ye well!"

Lissy peeked out from underneath her coat to see if the shadows had disappeared. *It worked!* she thought. But unfortunately the moon's light faded with them as the clouds covered its face and it was dark once more.

The wind picked up and the trees rocked and swayed. Branches cracked and popped, and dart-like snowflakes poked her skin. In the distance she heard the eerie laughing

14

and yipping howl of coyotes. Her heart pounded like it would leap from her chest. Every time she took a breath she was sure that the coyotes would hear it. She was afraid they were coming for her and wanted to cry, but they would hear that, too. That helpless feeling came over her once again. The trees seemed to sense her desperation and wrapped their limbs around her protectively. Snow came from every direction, blinding her.

The howling filled her mind along with the voice of one of her brother's favorite stinging insults, *"Now you've really done it, Geek."*

CHAPTER FOUR – The Finding

Panic swept over Lissy like wild fire. She wanted Los Angelees, her Grandma, even her own family. She wanted anything, anyone. She wanted to be anywhere other than here—in the woods, in a snowstorm, in the middle of the night, alone. The distant howling carried to her on the icy wind and sounded clearer and closer, clawing its way through the thick canopy. She started to climb into the branches of the pine. Pulling her woolen stockings up to stay warm, she climbed the ladder-like branches higher. The tree rocked her in its arms like her Grandma once had and seemed to be whispering to her, singing. Lissy couldn't believe her ears. She actually started to make out the trees' strange words as they murmured among themselves. It was as if each tree passed on a message from one to the other.

"Deep in the heart of the Popple-Pine forest,
On a limb not far off the ground.
Come at once Twiggedy-Jig,
A child waits to be found."

Lissy swayed in time to the pine song and mumbled the words along with them. She didn't know what a "twiggedy jig" was, and hoped with all of her heart that it wasn't a troll or monster. But she did know that she trusted the trees and that she needed to be found soon.

"Twiggedy, Twiggedy, Twiggedy-Jig,
A child awaits you, come Twiggedy-Jig."

The wind cut through her coat like a knife. Lissy closed her eyes tightly and held the trunk of the tree with her mittened hand. She sang the rhyme with the trees, over and over, louder and faster. The howling, now coming from many different directions, formed a strange chorus as Lissy's desperate song combined with the voices of the trees and the wind.

From somewhere on the ground below her, Lissy heard a crashing sound. "Twiggedy, Twiggedy, Twiggedy-Jig, *please!"* she screamed.

She felt a tugging at the branch her feet rested on, and waited for the tearing and ripping of wild fangs. She opened one eye, expecting to see gaping jaws full of razor-sharp teeth and oozing long strings of drool.

17

Instead, she saw the flickering light of a small lantern and looked into the large, dark eyes of a very strange and very small old woman.

"Hurry child, they are nearly upon us! We must move quickly!" said the old woman, tugging at her feet.

Thankful for her rescuer, Lissy slid out of the branches, her teeth chattering and her short brown hair glued to her face by tears and snow. The old woman grabbed her mittened hand and pulled her through the trees. Lissy had no choice but to follow. Cold and exhausted, she trusted the old woman completely, not knowing where she was going or with whom.

The howling was closer now, just behind them and growing nearer. The old woman held the lantern higher and picked up the pace. Lissy noticed that the pine trees opened their arms wide for them to pass, and then locked down firmly in place after they stepped through, as if to protect them. The howling seemed further away now.

"Who-who are you?" Lissy asked as they slowed down a bit. The old woman turned, her shawl wrapped about her, and blew out the lantern.

"Why, don't you know child? You called me. I'm Twiggedy-Jig."

CHAPTER FIVE – Twiggedy-Jig

"We must be quiet now child, as the shadow dancers are still about. There will be time for questions later. We must get home quickly, without them seeing us." Lissy felt the old woman squeeze her hand and pull her through the trees. They zigged and zagged through the forest and the great pine branches swept the ground behind them, erasing their trail from the snow. They walked and walked until Lissy felt that she could not take another step.

"Well, here we are and here we be," said Twiggedy, as she came to the foot of a large maple tree. Hidden on the other side of the tree was a small door. Twiggedy lead Lissy in and shut the door behind them.

Lissy stood in amazement and wonder as she looked about the room while the little old woman, smaller than she, bustled about preparing a fire and place for her to sit. She led Lissy over to the stone hearth and sat her down upon a stool, pulled off her one mitten and placed it carefully on the table. She was strangely dressed—she wore a long, dark, full skirt with a shawl wrapped around her shoulders and her hair held up in a red scarf. Definitely not what a proper woman would wear.

"Take off you coat, deary, and your shoes, mind you. And don't forget your stockings," Twiggedy said, stirring the contents of a small, black kettle over the fire. Lissy shivered in her thin, pink dress and bloomers. Twiggedy fetched a warm blanket and handed it to Lissy. "Give them here." She nodded to Lissy's wet clothing. Shyly, she handed her things to the old woman and wrapped the warm blanket tightly around her.

"How did you know where I was?" Lissy asked through chattering teeth.

"Oh, a little bird told me," said Twiggedy-Jig. Lissy watched with interest as the strange, old woman busied herself near the fire.

"Are you an *angel?*" Lissy asked shyly.

Twiggedy's laugh was like a bubbling brook—warm, familiar and comforting. "No, my child, I'm not an angel," she said, tapping a ladle on the side of the kettle.

"Then are you a *gypsy?* Mother told me to beware of the gypsy women. They steal away children in the night," Lissy said, worrying for the first time that maybe the little old woman might be dangerous. Twiggedy squealed with laughter, unlike the mocking laughter Lissy was used to in her family. "A gypsy!? My lands and my sake, goodness child, no," she said, ladling hot liquid into two cups.

Lissy breathed a sigh of relief.

Twiggedy smiled, her dark eyes catching the light. As she handed Lissy the steaming cup to drink she said, "Child, I'm a witch."

CHAPTER SIX – The Old Wood Witch

"A *witch*!" Lissy almost dropped the warm cup. She looked down at the drink in her hands with the horrible thought that the old woman brought her back here to fatten her up and devour her, just like in all of the storybooks. *A witch was much worse than a gypsy!* Everyone knew that witches ate children, like Hansel and Gretel.

"A witch is the *worst* thing anyone can be!" Lissy was choked with fear, her blue eyes wide with fright.

"Tsk, tsk, tsk, child. My stars, where did you *ever* get an idea like that?"

"My mother said so. She said that witches fly with

the devil and do his bidding," Lissy said, pulling her blanket higher about her face.

"Hmmm," Twiggedy said, "maybe you shouldn't believe everything you hear."

"Are you going to *eat* me?" Lissy finally blurted out, wanting to get it over with.

"No, child, not today," Twiggedy said, chuckling heartily. "Wait until I tell the girls *that* one!" Then she added, "No child, never. I'm Twiggedy-Jig, the old witch of the wood. I find lost children and care for the forest and animals and such."

"So this isn't a magic potion to poison me?" asked Lissy, relaxing a little.

"Child, no," Twiggedy assured her, "it's just spiced apple cider to warm your bones, now drink up." Twiggedy smiled warmly at her and spoke to something in the corner, "Strange little lamb indeed, Dee-Dee."

Perched on an old cuckoo clock in the corner was a fluff-ball of a bird. Lissy was sure that it was the chickadee that led her to the pine shelter. It winked at Lissy and tucked its head back into the warmth of its feathers. "Good idea, Dee-Dee, its been a long night and we all need our rest," said Twiggedy, pulling down the thick covers of a tiny bed for Lissy.

The soft bed and the warm, spicy drink seemed so inviting to Lissy that, at this point, she didn't even *care* if the wood witch was going to eat her. So she drank the sweet cider (that did, in fact, warm her right down to her bones), climbed into the bed, pulled the pine-scented covers up to her chin, and then nodded off to sleep.

Twiggedy hobbled over to the clock, pulled the chain to wind it and returned to the hearth, where she sat by the fire stirring the red coals.

"Sleep little one, for tomorrow will be an even bigger day," she said, shaking her head and humming a little song, as Lissy fell into a deep, restful sleep.

Lissy dreamed that she was back at home in her own bed, safe and sound. Her Grandma was asleep in the chair, snoring softly, the "good book" in her lap. Lissy heard the creak of her bedroom door opening and her heart jumped into her throat as someone entered the room. It wasn't her father, or her mother. She thought that maybe it was her brother, sneaking in to play a trick on her, but realized the shadow was taller than he was. It glided across the floor without a sound. The shadow moved to Lissy's dresser where her jewelry box sat. The shadow opened the box, pulled out a silver necklace with a crystal teardrop and stuffed it into a bag. Then the figure began to turn around. Lissy was terrified.

Before her stood an old Indian woman, her silver and black hair tied back tightly. She wore a long, black, net-like shawl that seemed to drink in the darkness. The pearls on the woman's many necklaces tinkled lightly as she turned to look at Lissy. Her gaze was like that of a cat ready to pounce upon a bird, and she grinned crookedly. She disappeared as Lissy blinked her eyes.

Lissy sat up in bed, trembling. "Grandma! Did you see her? She was here!"

Twiggedy stirred in her chair. The pale, pink light of dawn crept into the strange room. The fire crackled softly. The clock ticked steadily on the wall.

Lissy looked around. This wasn't her room. And that wasn't her Grandma sitting in the corner. Outside, the wind howled and snowflakes tapped at the tiny, round window. "What did you say dear?" Twiggedy asked groggily as she stood up and stretched.

"I-I had a bad dream," Lissy said, confused. "I-I thought, I dreamed, that someone came in, but I was in my bed, at home."

Twiggedy was fully awake now. Lissy pulled the covers around her shoulders as the little bird fluttered awake, too.

Twiggedy stoked the fire and put on a kettle to boil. She shook out Lissy's dress, bloomers, and stockings and handed them to her. Lissy's wool stockings were warm and dry, so she pulled them on first. She dressed in silence as Twiggedy went about making breakfast.

"Tell me, dear Elizabeth, what else was in your dream?" Twiggedy asked, taking down a plate of biscuits.

"Why did you call me Elizabeth? My name is Lissy. Besides, I never even *told* you my name," she said, now thoroughly confused.

"Well, if you prefer Lissy then, dear, that's fine," said Twiggedy, warming honey in a pot.

Lissy, feeling uneasy, hesitated, but then continued her dream story.

"There was an old Indian woman, and she came in and stole a crystal pendant necklace of mine from my jewelry box. Funny, I didn't know I had a necklace like that. But she took it, looked right at me, and then she left."

Twiggedy scowled, clucking her tongue as she went to the door. Faint, wet tracks led outside. "I don't think it was a dream you had, child. It looks like we had an uninvited guest last night."

Sunlight streamed in through the tiny, oval window and Lissy walked over to the puddle on the floor.

"Oh, dear, this is much worse than I thought," said Twiggedy as she stood in the morning light, studying Lissy up and down, front to back.

"Why do you say that?" Lissy asked, looking down at her hands and feet.

"Child, can't you *see*? Your *shadow* is missing!"

CHAPTER SEVEN – Shadow Chaser

Things were rapidly becoming too much for Lissy. She stood there in the rosy sunlight and wailed.

"Not only am I lost and in a witch's lair, but I've even managed to lose my own shadow!" Lissy turned to look behind her and found nothing.

"There, there dear. I realize you *are* in a bit of spot, but old Twiggedy will help you," Twiggedy said, trying to comfort poor Lissy. She sat her down and gave her a cup of warm chamomile tea. Lissy looked into the cup and watched as tears dripped into the steaming yellow liquid.

"Even ants have shadows. I'm smaller than an ant—I'm nothing," Lissy whimpered.

"Well then, you *are* in bad shape, child," said Twiggedy. "Here now, drink this and you'll feel better."

"Thank you. My very own dear Grandma used to give me chamomile tea when I was upset," Lissy sniffed.

Twiggedy sat the plate of warmed biscuits and honey before her. "Eat up, dear."

Lissy cautiously tasted one biscuit, then ate the others with gusto.

"You may have lost your shadow, but you haven't lost your appetite," Twiggedy said, chuckling and slapping her thigh.

"How can you laugh at me?" Feeling sorry for herself, Lissy's eyes welled up again.

"Oh, don't fret, we'll get your old shadow back and you'll be good as new," Twiggedy said sympathetically. "Now then, seeing as you are new to these woods there are some things you should know. Since your shadow is missing, you won't be able to leave the house. You are only half a person now," Twiggedy said, sipping her tea.

"You mean I can't even go out and look for my family? They'll be worried sick about me!" Lissy's headed drooped. *"Well, maybe."*

"Without your shadow you can't go back home, dear. You are vulnerable now—Shadow Chaser might come back for you."

"For me? It already has my shadow, what else would it want?" Lissy suddenly grew cold.

"Why, your breath, dear, your life—that's what you

have left." Twiggedy stared at Lissy. "However, Shadow Chaser may be happy with just your shadow for now. Chances are she won't be looking in the heavier snows of winter. She may toy with you and wait until the spring thaw," Twiggedy said, rubbing her chin and concocting a plan. "You must stay here in the house and let my friends and me help you."

"You *have* to get my shadow back for me, it's been with me all my life!" Lissy said, her reddened eyes pleading. "It looks just like me, only taller with longer, darker hair and it wears a long, blue velvet dress. Do you really think you can find it?"

Twiggedy looked up at the clock on the wall, and clucked her tongue. "Yes, child, soon. When the time is right."

Dee-Dee hopped to the table for biscuit crumbs, then fluttered from the chair to the door handle. Twiggedy let the little bird outside and sat down at the table with her cup of tea.

"We have plenty of time to find your shadow, but you need to tell me *everything* that happened last night," Twiggedy said, gazing into her tea and stirring it.

"Well, my family came to the cabin on the lake to close it up for winter and to get away after, you know..." started Lissy.

"Your grandmother's death, child?" Twiggedy asked softly, patting Lissy's hand.

"Yes, that," she answered looking down, "and I left my book on the table and we left and then I fell out of the car."

"Ohhh, so you *jumped* out of the car." Twiggedy said. She clucked her tongue again and shook her head sadly. "Dear, dear me."

"No! I didn't jump and I wasn't pushed! I simply fell out. It was an accident, you see," Lissy said impatiently.

"Hmmm," Twiggedy rubbed her chin and looked out the window, "there are no accidents, child. In life you choose—you choose to be in a car, or not to be in a car. You chose not to be."

Lissy felt as tiny and helpless as a mouse cornered by a cat. She thought really hard and she was pretty sure that she fell out, but supposed that she could she have jumped like the old woman said.

"I didn't do anything wrong," Lissy said in a small voice. Then she remembered her wish at the lake and suddenly she felt quite ill and her cheeks burned.

"Oh my," Twiggedy said, setting down her tea. "You made a wish, did you? This does change things. Child, when you made the wish you invited adventure to come find you."

"So, how did I lose my shadow?"

"The bump on the road must have loosened it some. It happens." Twiggedy said, casually wiping crumbs into her hand.

"I didn't know that things like this happened. Why didn't anyone ever tell me?" Lissy felt embarrassed and a little angry.

"Think about it. How did you feel after your fall?" Twiggedy prodded.

"Well, I did feel funny, and I heard things, like the

trees…" Lissy started, but was afraid to continue for fear of the old woman laughing at her like her own family typically did.

"Go on, child," Twiggedy reassured her.

"Well, I heard the trees singing. I thought it was the wind at first, but they sang such a lovely song that I started to sing along with them. Then you found me."

"You *called* me," Twiggedy corrected Lissy. "And you *did* hear the trees talking. They talk amongst themselves and they sing, too. Their voices can travel great distances, and from one tree to the next, the message is delivered," Twiggedy continued. "Once someone loses their shadow, they begin hearing the voices of many things they never heard before," Twiggedy said, "and they *see* things, too."

Twiggedy got up and cleared the table. For the first time since she arrived, Lissy really looked at the strange, little house. The large clock on the wall was much like the cuckoo clock her uncle had—the kind with deer, birds, and squirrels chasing each other around it, all carved of dark wood. She noticed that the clock ticked, but the little bird didn't come out. Perhaps it was broken. After all, living out here in the middle of the forest, one may not have a clock tinker about. She looked closer at the clock and saw that it only had one hand and eight carved symbols rather than numerals on the face. Twiggedy answered her question before she had asked it: "It tells the seasons."

Lissy looked at the walls and noticed that there was no wallpaper like she had at home. She got up and touched the walls of the round room. They were rough, like a log, and there were knotholes in them.

"It's maple," said Twiggedy, clearing her throat.

"Oh," said Lissy, "it almost looks like…"

"Yes dear, I live in a tree," Twiggedy said softly, as she poured water into a bucket and wiggled her middle finger over the top of it as if she were stirring.

"How can anyone live in a tree?" Lissy asked with wide eyes, as steam slowly rose from the bucket.

"Things are not the same anymore," Twiggedy said dropping the breakfast dishes into the steaming water. "There are things you will soon find out." After testing the water she handed Lissy a dishrag. Twiggedy smiled at her as she gathered some cloth bags from the cupboard.

"*One* of those things," Twiggedy said with a twinkle in her eye, "is that I can change my appearance." She took the empty bags, wrapped her cloak about her and opened the door, allowing golden morning sunlight and sparkling snowflakes to swirl inside.

Lissy heard what Twiggedy had said, but she still didn't expect what happened next. Before her very eyes, the kindly old woman in her worn, black cloak turned into a prickly, bristly porcupine.

32

CHAPTER EIGHT – The Cupboard

Lissy watched Twiggedy, as an old porcupine, waddle off through the trees. The little chickadee, Dee-Dee, flew to the door and scolded the girl, cocking its black eye at her as if to say she must stay inside. Lissy recited:

"A birdie with a yellow bill,
Hopped upon the window sill.
Cocked its shining eye and said,
"'Ain't you shamed you sleepy head?'"

She closed the door and watched the bird flit over and perch on the knob of the cupboard. "You must be Twiggedy's watch bird," she laughed.

"I guess she's not so bad—*for a witch*," Lissy said to the bird as she washed the cups and plate in the bucket of warm water. She dried the dishes, made up the bed and dusted the clock to surprise the old woman.

When she finished with her chores the sun was high overhead. Twiggedy still had not returned. Bored, Lissy began to investigate the tiny house. She came across a staircase that she hadn't noticed before. The steps wound in a spiral, high up into the tree. She peered up toward the top and could see light coming in from another oval window. Dee-Dee flitted and fluttered about her face. "Oh, all right, another time I guess," Lissy said as she went back to the cupboard to put the dishes away.

"Top or bottom, which will it be, Dee-Dee?" Lissy laughed and opened the doors at the bottom. Pots and jars and extra blankets filled the shelves, leaving no room for the dishes. By now, Lissy was getting hungry again and searched the bottom cupboard hoping to find some cookies. She opened a small, unmarked jar and took a whiff. Sweet smelling herbs tickled her nose. Then she opened another labeled "Dried Cranberries" and nibbled on those. They were sweet, yet sour, and quite tasty, but now she was curious and thought there might be other good things to eat.

She proceeded to open the largest canister labeled "S. Cabbage."

"Oh! This must be steamed cabbage! How I loved

Grandma's cooked cabbage!" she said to the now frantic bird. The canister was difficult to open, so she put all of her strength into it. The top popped off like a cannon and out burst the foulest odor Lissy had ever smelled. An aroma of freshly sprayed skunk filled the tiny room, knocking her over backwards, coughing and choking. She scrambled to replace the lid on the jar of Skunk Cabbage and put the jars back into the cupboard.

Next, Lissy opened the top doors and when she did, Dee-Dee flew about the room excitedly and chirped. She found a large book of birch bark pages, several bottles of ink, a bunch of feathers, and some big jars toward the back. Thinking that Twiggedy may have cookies hidden in the back like her mother did at home, Lissy reached past everything to grab the green glass jar.

The jar was heavy and was filled with strange things. She carried it over to the table to better examine the contents. Instead of the cookies she had hoped for, the jar was filled with bones! Lissy jumped back in horror and nearly fainted.

Once again, she felt like a small animal, cornered and frightened. She had forgotten that the old woman was really a witch. What if these were the bones of children she had found! Did she eat them and save the bones for her magic? After all, the old woman did tell her not to believe everything she heard. Lissy panicked and ran to get her coat. She flung the door open and nearly ran into Twiggedy, who was struggling to hold the bags she'd filled while she was out.

"Oh, thank you dear, just put these on the table,"

Twiggedy said, her dark eyes smiling. She thrust the bags into Lissy's hands. A strange, musty odor was oozing from the bags. Twiggedy closed the door and stepped inside. She shook out her cape and hung it near the fire. Lissy stood frozen, unable to move.

"Just set them on the table, dear," Twiggedy repeated, stirring the fire.

Lissy, still in shock and her arms loaded with the smelly bags, blurted out, "Are there dead things in these?"

Twiggedy turned around to face the frightened child. Dee-Dee landed on her red scarf and chipped into her ear.

"Hmm," Twiggedy said with a frown, "someone has been snooping around, I hear."

Lissy dropped the bags onto the table and a pile of grayish-brown things tumbled out. They looked like old ears, all dried up and wrinkled. Lissy backed up toward the door. "I-I'm sorry, I was bored and hungry, so I was looking around a bit, and I...I didn't mean to find your jar of dead children parts!"

Twiggedy's face went blank for a moment and Lissy's heart seemed to stop. She didn't know if the old woman would come across the table and beat her or just end it all right here and now and pop her into the stew.

Twiggedy stammered, "Dead children parts?" Then she bent over, laughing and coughing, and slapped the table. "Child, you *do* have an imagination! I told you not to believe everything you hear."

Lissy didn't know if she should feel better or not. "But what about all those bones and these dried ears on the table?" she asked, pointing to the smelly pile.

"Those are dried mushrooms. I gathered them from my storage tree so I can prepare a protection spell for you."

"Are they poisonous?" Lissy asked, still not convinced that the old woman was trying to help her.

"No dear, I eat mushrooms all the time. I know which ones are good and which are bad," Twiggedy said.

"Do you use them in bad spells to hurt people?"

"My dear," Twiggedy said with a stern seriousness, "no one should *ever* harm another. Our magic is used for the good of all, to make life better, not to be hurtful to others."

The old woman's eyes suddenly changed and became like those of an animal, intense and powerful, and she said, "*For whatever one puts out, comes back times three.*" Lissy knew that even though she was an old woman, she was someone not to be crossed. She believed Twiggedy would cause her no harm and she relaxed. Dee-Dee flitted to the clock and swung from it upside down by her toes. Her silly antics cleared the air, and soon both Lissy and Twiggedy were laughing.

"Looks like someone else is hungry, too," Twiggedy said in her usual friendly tone. "We have much cooking to do before sundown."

CHAPTER NINE – The Spell

"So then, why do you have all those bones and things in the cupboard?" Lissy asked.

"Well, it's quite a long story, but the short of it is, I make dolls to protect the forest from intruders up to no good. I have done this for a long time now. My grandmother taught me, as did hers before her. I come from a long line of wood witches," she said proudly.

"What do you do with these dolls?" Lissy asked, remembering her own beloved Los Angelees. "Do you *play* with them?"

"No. I gather up bones, feathers and such things that

I find in the woods. Each piece belongs to a particular plant or animal—all a part of the forest. Then I put them together and send them out on the night of a full moon, where they come to life and dance through the forest, doing their work. Some sing songs that lighten the hearts of kind people, while others may be sneaky and scare off those wishing to do harm. Some people call them sprites, 'kobold,' or the 'little people.' But I call them my little helpers," Twiggedy said with a wink.

"I've had dolls, too. My first was a rubber doll named Toodles," Lissy spoke softly, "and then there was Los Angelees." Lissy paused, looking up at the old woman to see if she would laugh at the name, like her family had.

"Oh, what a *beautiful* name for a beloved doll!" Twiggedy's eyes glowed with excitement as she chopped the mushrooms.

Lissy brightened, "You really like it? Her name, Los Angelees? You don't think it's strange?"

"Oh, child, the name means *'of the angels',*" Twiggedy said, smiling warmly.

Lissy thought that her heart would burst with pride.

"Could you please make me a doll someday, Twiggedy? I so miss Los Angelees, and you could even make her come to life. I have always wanted a little sister," Lissy said, her gray-blue eyes getting teary.

"Perhaps one day, dear, when the time is right," Twiggedy said patting her hand. "But right now we have work to do."

The sun was near setting as Twiggedy prepared the table with a variety of mushroom platters and warm bread and butter. Lissy stood on one side of the table and the old woman on the other. The last rays of orange light settled on them as Twiggedy lit a black candle. Lissy watched and listened to the silence of twilight and the candle spitting. The candle flickered and cast shadows about the walls.

Twiggedy instructed Lissy to throw some salt around her in a circle. After she did this, they stood in readiness. Twiggedy lit a sprig of cedar and placed it in a bowl. She wafted the smoke toward her face and spoke these words:

"Mushrooms that grow on decaying matter,
food of fungus on this platter.
Mask this child in death's smell,
trick the senses of prey beast well."

With that, Twiggedy looked up at Lissy, grinning, and announced, "So it be done! Let's eat!" The two laughed and sat down to the table set with the fungal feast.

Lissy started with creamed mushroom soup and some mushroom bread with mushroom cheese. She found these delicious and moved on to the mushrooms-fried-like-steaks and mushrooms-stuffed-like-potatoes. These were quite tasty, too. But when it was time for dessert, mushroom kabobs in maple syrup and cream, she decided that she'd had enough. She sipped some hot spruce needle tea and belched loudly.

"Excuse me. Is the spell done? Because I am feeling rather puffy right now," Lissy said, leaning back and holding her stomach with her hands.

"For now," said Twiggedy, as she finished her meal with Dee-Dee on her shoulder, "but you must eat them everyday, at every meal, for it to work its best."

Lissy looked down at her plate and watched a big tear plop onto a mushroom crumb, as she said in a small voice, "Every *day?*"

CHAPTER TEN – Magic

Every day Lissy cleaned the little house and did her chores and looked out the window at the silent, snowy-white world. Never once did she hear the clock's cuckoo bird come out to announce the season. Lissy had become accustomed to Twiggedy changing into her porcupine shape and waddling out for firewood everyday, and would wait by the door and watch for her return, being careful not to step on a stray, sharp quill. She played fetch with Dee-Dee and hopscotch near the fire. But today Lissy was unusually lonely for home, and even the small mice babies that she had found tucked in a nest under the cupboard didn't seem to lift her spirits.

By now it would be Christmas, and she dreamed of flaming plum puddings and crispy, golden turkey. Packages wrapped in bright paper, strings of popcorn, and scarlet cranberries would decorate the tall, fragrant fir tree. It was her favorite time of the year, when all the family gathered to sing and play, and she actually felt loved. Her Aunt Tootsie and Aunt Mimsy visited then. Both were nurses, and both were funny and eccentric, but that's where the similarity ended. Tootsie had dark hair and playful brown eyes and loved to laugh, where Mimsy was more prim and proper, an elegant blonde with bright, blue eyes. How Lissy missed Tootsie's game of teasing her sister to make her angry! Mimsy would pretend to be angry and then laugh in her gentle bubbling way. It was hard to believe that the two were sisters.

Lissy's Grandpa Brown gave her sweet, pink mints that melted in her mouth, and she would step onto the toes of his big, black shoes and they would dance around the tree.

She thought of her Uncle Ward, smartly dressed and smelling of cologne, bringing them ice cream and lemon sodas. She remembered that special Christmas when he handed her the large present with the red wrapping paper and the silver bow, and how she felt when she opened the box and set eyes on her doll, Los Angelees. Her heart ached for those wonderful times and especially for her beloved doll.

Humming to the baby mice, she strung a piece of yarn around their nest and placed them snugly in the corner by the fireplace. She took down a small sprig of club moss and propped it up next to them for their Christmas tree. It was then that she had an idea. Twiggedy had been much too busy to make Lissy a doll, so she would just use some of Twiggedy's things to make her own doll! Her spirits soared at the thought.

Lissy pulled down the scraps from the cupboard and laid things out on the table as Dee-Dee bounced about. Twiggedy wouldn't be back for hours so she had plenty of time before she had to put supper on.

She found scraps of bright, colorful blanket material, corn husks and some little seeds for eyes and teeth. She instantly felt very cheery and sang Christmas songs while she worked. She would no longer be lonely! Soon she would have a friend to cuddle—maybe even two, if there was time.

She felt around in a deep canister and pulled out two roots that looked like doll bodies. They were exactly what she needed. She laughed at her good fortune but Dee-Dee hopped from chair to table to cupboard, scolding her.

"Twiggedy won't mind, Dee-Dee," Lissy said, working on the doll's faces. She tried to fix the hair but it kept sticking up. The teeth were a little crooked and one eye was bigger than the other and crossed a bit, but she loved the strange-looking little thing. The doll reminded her of her own self, imperfect and a little bit raggedy.

She thought the other doll's face would be better, but it turned out looking mean and a little scary. The harder she tried, the more frustrated she grew and eventually she thought it would just have to be good enough the way it was.

When Lissy decided she was through, she looked out at the sun dropping behind the trees and announced to her dolls, "Tea time!"

She cleaned up her supplies and sat the dolls at the table. She set out little cups for all of them, even a cup for Dee-Dee who hopped about nervously.

"One lump or two?" she asked the dolls, pretending to put sugar cubes into their cups. But they didn't answer her. *"Oh bother, and oh shoe, listen when I talk to you!"* Lissy laughed at her little rhyme—she sounded just like Twiggedy! "Now, one lump or two?" she asked her doll guests again.

Then, to Lissy's surprise, up jumped the angry-looking doll who replied, "None for me, but two for you!" Lissy ducked just in time, as he threw both teacups aimed straight at her head.

She watched in shock as the other doll came to life in the dying pink sunlight. They ran about the room, chasing poor Dee-Dee and smashing things. The cross-eyed doll laughed and chanted, *"Tea for two, tea for two!"* He clapped his hands and danced about the room, running into things and bouncing off the walls.

Now she had really done it! Dishes flew around the room and ashes scattered from the fireplace settled over everything like snowflakes. Lissy ran to the door, choking, and jerked it open as the two mischievous idiots ran past her and out into the forest, whooping and hollering and kicking up their heels. She slammed the door shut and turned to look at the mess. Her heart sank. Then she remembered Twiggedy would be home soon and she started cleaning up.

Just as she had swept up the last of the ashes, the door opened. The look on Twiggedy's face told Lissy that something was wrong. She hoped that Twiggedy wouldn't discover what had happened.

"Hmmm," Twiggedy grunted as she lay the firewood down by the door. She turned to shake her cloak and hung it to dry. She sat down at the table and Lissy handed her a cup of warm tea.

"Seems a little weak," Twiggedy said, annoyed, sipping her drink. Lissy gulped and set the table for dinner, noisily clattering the plates and silver.

"Someone has something to tell me?" Twiggedy said staring out the window. "Was someone careless today?"

"I was lonely," Lissy said in a tiny voice, dishing up her mushroom stew.

"Magic is not a game," Twiggedy said, squinting at her. "You must take great care. You must remember to be careful what you wish for, because you just may get it. And most importantly, you must be mindful to guard your thoughts while you make something, because it will show in your work."

Twiggedy pulled the two dolls out of her bag and laid them on the table. Their blank, dark eyes stared up accusingly at Lissy. She jumped back in alarm but they weren't alive now. They were tattered and torn from their first and last romp of freedom.

CHAPTER ELEVEN – Twiggedy's Surprise

Though the days gradually got longer, Lissy was still lonely. Twiggedy-Jig spent hours out in the forest caring for animals and trees and gathering things. Then she'd appear in the little house, seemingly out of nowhere. Lissy had been cooped up for three full months, and thankfully, there had been no sign of the Shadow Chaser.

Now Twiggedy would let her outside for a bit, as long as she didn't stray too far.

Lissy loved bundling up and being in the sunshine and exploring her forest home. All around her, the trees popped and cracked from the cold like popcorn in a pan. Occasionally, she would turn to look back behind her, in hopes of seeing her shadow. She wished that Twiggedy would find it soon, for she missed dancing with it.

Wandering about from tree to tree, she noticed a funny knot on one that looked like a face. She stopped to brush the snow away and pulled off her mitten to feel the rough silver bark, when the eyes of the tree slowly opened. It looked like someone stirring in his sleep.

"It has always been my experience that when one gets too tall, one will someday topple," the big poplar said to Lissy, then went back to sleep. Lissy was surprised and a bit flustered by this exchange and looked at her hand and then back at the sleeping tree.

She continued walking along and stopped to feel each tree. The soft, smooth flesh of a birch shivered when Lissy touched it. She thought she had better let the trees sleep since they had a lot of work to do in the spring. She went back into the house to warm her feet by the fire.

The clock on the wall ticked away, but still would not cuckoo. This bothered Lissy. Sometimes she thought she might try to repair it herself but Dee-Dee would fly around in agitation if Lissy even got *near* the clock, and, after the doll incident, she felt it best if she just let it be. So today she thought she would climb the stairs and see what was up there. Dee-Dee was snoozing on the cupboard, a place where she often rested, as if guarding its contents.

Lissy sneaked onto the first few steps then squeezed her way up. The stairway became smaller and tighter as it spiraled up the tree trunk. When she finally reached the top, she saw the little oval window. She looked out at the frosty, sparkling world below and was awed by the sight.

The purple, shadowy fingers stretching across the snow seemed to tickle the trees. As she watched birds winding up and down tree trunks in search of juicy insects, she felt bad for Dee-Dee, who had to stay with Lissy instead of flitting about with her friends. She soon forgot about that and she laughed at the black squirrels' noisy game of tag and watched a deer twitch its ears in the distance. This was the best time she'd had in a long while.

Then she spotted a large, black woodpecker with a long, red crest. It was the most beautiful, and by far the biggest, woodpecker she had ever seen. Like Lissy had earlier, it too went from tree to tree, knocking and tapping. She became so enchanted, watching the bird, that she was stunned when it flew straight to the window where Lissy stood. She stepped back and nearly tumbled down the steps as the large, black wings came through the opening. Lissy blinked and found herself looking right into Twiggedy's large, dark eyes.

"Oh, child, you frightened me!" Twiggedy gasped.

"Frightened *you?* Lissy exclaimed, following Twiggedy down the narrow steps. "I didn't know you could fly!"

"Many things you don't know," Twiggedy laughed.

The next day Twiggedy was busier than usual. She hummed as she prepared food and cleaned. The snow outside had started melting, which was good for the forest world, but worried Lissy as she thought about the Shadow Chaser coming for her. They cleaned the house from top to bottom.

Lissy washed her wool stockings and hung them to dry and was shaking out her heavy coat when the little red canoe popped out and clattered across the floor. She had forgotten all about the canoe that she found at the lake. It seemed so long ago when her life had changed

Twiggedy walked over and picked it up, studied it and handed it to Lissy. Lissy held the small canoe up to the light and inspected it again. It was still the same as the day she found it, even the fall from the car had not harmed it. She tucked the canoe carefully back into her pocket and patted it.

"Many things you don't know, either," Lissy said smartly, bothered by Twiggedy keeping secrets from her.

"Hmmm," was all Twiggedy said. By now, Lissy knew that when Twiggedy sighed that way, she had more to say on the subject, but today they were much too busy to discuss it.

The next morning before sunrise, the sound of the cuckoo clock startled Lissy from sleep. "Dong-cuckoo, dong-cuckoo," it called in a metallic voice.

"It's half past winter and a quarter to spring!" Twiggedy announced, jumping up from bed. "Our guests will be arriving soon!"

"Guests? Who?" Lissy said, doubly dumbfounded between the clock's chiming and Twiggedy's announcement.

"Two of my very best friends," Twiggedy said cheerily. "We visit each other every so often, and also, when we have *wood spells* to do."

CHAPTER TWELVE – The Visit

As Lissy dressed for the day, she became a little nervous over the thought of guests arriving. Her pink dress, she had noticed, was losing its color and became more faded and ragged each day. She hoped that Twiggedy had noticed, too, so that she might do something about it. Her shoes pinched her feet slightly and her bangs had started to grow over eyes.

"We'll take care of that dear," Twiggedy said, reading Lissy's mind. "But now we must put the pot on to boil."

An excited Dee-Dee fluttered about so much that Twiggedy finally let the chattering bird outside, where she disappeared into the sunlit woods.

"May I go upstairs now and watch for our guests?" asked Lissy.

"Go on, child, everything is set," Twiggedy said as she prepared a fragrant tea of rose hips and spruce needles.

Lissy climbed the winding stairs to her favorite spot by the window and sat with her head in her hands looking out with great wonder at the world below. She sighed at the beauty of morning in the forest and inhaled the fresh air. She had grown accustomed to calling to the animals and birds as they passed by each day. Now with her hair growing longer, she daydreamed that she was Rapunzel, held prisoner in her high tower awaiting her prince.

The sun had warmed the squirrels to activity and they chased each other up and down the trees. Three does walked along their worn trail and stopped to listen, with their ears held high, their wet, black noses sniffed the air. When they were satisfied there was no danger, they resumed looking for missed acorns and whatever they could find for breakfast. Woodpeckers, smartly dressed in their black-and-white-checkered suits, rat-a-tat-tatted on the trunks of birch and maple.

Her favorite bird, the nuthatch, hopped upside-down honking like the horn on a bicycle. Twiggedy said they find things that the other birds miss by looking at the world differently. So Lissy tried to look at the world differently too, and attempted twisting her head upside-down to look up.

In the distance, she noticed a small, gray thing trudging through the snow. The creature waddled, then stopped, and waddled then stopped and looked up at Lissy. It was an opossum. It lifted its naked tail high so as not to drag it in the snow. Its pink feet stuck out beneath what looked like Lissy's own black leggings, and they looked cold and sore. *Poor thing needs some gloves*, Lissy thought.

The deer lifted their heads, looked at the opossum, then went back to dining. Just then Dee-Dee flew in through the window and flitted about the room, all a-twitter.

"Our guest has arrived!" Twiggedy called from below. But Lissy never saw anyone come up to the house. In fact, the only thing near the door was the poor, cold opossum. She climbed back down as Twiggedy opened the door to greet her guest.

"Well, land sakes and bless my soul! Gerty dear, come in, come in," Twiggedy laughed, filling the doorway. Dee-Dee bounced about excitedly like a dog upon seeing the visitor.

Lissy still didn't see anyone. Suddenly a small woman in a large, straw hat with a basket on her arm stood in the doorway. She wore a silver shawl pulled about her black blouse and a long, gray skirt. She was a bit younger than Twiggedy, and she had ice-blue eyes that sparkled and a shy, kindly smile.

"Oh, I see you have company, Twiggedy," the little woman said, her voice soft and musical.

"My yes, Gerty. This is Lissy, she's staying with us for a while," Twiggedy said, taking her shawl. Gerty placed the basket on the table and rubbed her cold, pink hands

54

together to warm them. Lissy looked at the woman and thought she seemed oddly familiar.

"We've already met," she said to Lissy, who was greatly confused. "In the window, that is." She winked at Lissy and said "I'm Gerty Goodapple. I live in the old orchards, quite a distance from here," Twiggedy came over with a cup of tea for Gerty to warm her hands on.

"Goodness, thank you dear," Gerty said, blowing at the steam.

"Twiggedy, I thought you said that we were expecting *guests*," Lissy whispered shyly.

"Yes dear, it takes Rosemary a little longer to arrive. Her stiff joints and all," Twiggedy said chuckling.

"Now, Twiggedy," Gerty criticized, "don't you make excuses for Rose, you know how she gets distracted and forgets about time."

"Hmm, yes," Twiggedy said, and they laughed together heartily. Lissy touched the light-blue, flowered cloth that covered the basket and wondered about its contents. She was just about to ask Gerty what was inside when she heard a shuffling outside the door.

Twiggedy bustled over to open it. Standing there in the doorway was another small woman, not much older than Gerty. She seemed flustered and her large, dark eyes darted about under the brown cloak covering her head. Twiggedy chortled, hugging her visitor and clapping her on the back.

Gerty sat at the table sipping her tea as Twiggedy ushered her friend in and shut the door. The woman pulled off her thick cloak and handed it to Twiggedy. She wore a long, deep-blue dress, and embroidered leggings unlike anything Lissy had ever seen. She carried a beautifully beaded bag with tiny, tin cones that jingled and tinkled with her every movement. It was bulging and hung heavy on the woman's shoulder.

Preoccupied with settling into the little house, Rosemary suddenly stopped to look at Lissy through squinted eyes. She studied Lissy's face as if reading a book and tapped her lip, like she just remembered something to tell the child. Rosemary's look of mystery was soon forgotten as she burst into a warm smile that made Lissy's heart melt. For that fleeting instant, Lissy almost seemed to recognize the strange woman, but the memory slipped away like a little silver minnow.

The woman giggled like a young girl and rushed over to embrace Lissy. "I'm Bog-Rosemary, but you may call me Rose," she chattered excitedly.

"This is Lissy, Rose. She's staying with me for awhile," Twiggedy said, "Her family pushed her out of an automobile."

What was for a short time a warm, tender moment, now seemed uncomfortable and tense.

"No, I *fell* out," Lissy said defensively.

"Oh, well, then did you *jump* out, dear?" Gerty asked with a look of concern on her face.

"No, I *fell* out, it was an *accident!*" Lissy felt tears stinging her eyes at what seemed an embarrassing attack. Her lip trembled as the three women stared at her.

"Hmmm," they muttered in unison.

"She lost her shadow in the process, bumped loose,

56

and then taken in the night by Shadow Chaser," Twiggedy continued the story.

"Ahhh, a predicament indeed," clucked Gerty, shaking her head.

"Poor *dear,*" Rose said sniffing, with tears in her eyes.

"Well, enough on that matter!" Twiggedy interrupted, clapping her hands together sharply, "for we have gossip to catch up on and business to attend to." And just as suddenly, everyone came back to the happy occasion of being together.

The women chattered back and forth, laughing and drinking tea, eyes all aglow when Lissy asked, *"What business, Twiggedy?"*

"Oh, we must plan for the *Calling-of-the-Green* ceremony, dear," Twiggedy said casually, then went back to talking with her friends.

"What ceremony, Twiggedy?" Lissy asked.

"We witches gather at this time of the year to call the green back to the forest and field. The birds carry the warmth of the spring."

"You mean THEY are witches, *too?*" Lissy asked in a high voice, her eyes wide. They all put their cups down to stare at Lissy.

"Of *course*, dear," said Rose, smiling.

"Why, yes and there is much work to be done," Gerty laughed brightly.

Lissy's head reeled and her stomach rolled as she felt the familiar sense of panic wash over her. She was trapped again, and now she was outnumbered. Just like in the storybooks, Lissy had been Twiggedy's slave, cooking the meals and cleaning the house. And the storybooks told of witches laughing and flying through the night skies in search of children to eat. That must be why Twiggedy kept her here so long—they were going to feast upon her poor, wretched bones for their special ceremony!

Her heart jumped into her throat. Twiggedy had seemed a kindly old woman, even protecting Lissy with her spell. And all along, it was to keep Shadow Chaser away, so that Twiggedy would have Lissy all for her own!

Twiggedy stood up at the head of the table. As the shadows grew in the room behind her, she seemed large and menacing now—the leader of this wicked pack.

"We may as well get started, girls, before the ceremony and feast tomorrow," Twiggedy said as she pulled out a long, shiny knife.

Lissy jumped back against the cupboard, jarring its contents, which sent them rattling like wind chimes.

"Yes, perhaps we should begin now," Gerty said, standing up. She rummaged through her basket and pulled out a pair of sharp garden shears.

"Come here, child," Rose said as she held her hand out to Lissy. But that's all Lissy remembered, because right then, she fainted dead away.

CHAPTER THIRTEEN – The Party

"My land and my stars!" cried Twiggedy as she rushed to Lissy's side. The others bent over the girl in concern.

Lissy opened her eyes and let out a terrifying scream. All three women jumped back in alarm.

"Child, what has gotten in to you?" Twiggedy asked clutching her chest, her large eyes now even larger. "You frightened the stuffing out of me."

"Please, don't kill me and eat me! I'll be good and do whatever you want me to!" Lissy pleaded, looking up at them and sobbing.

"*Kill* you?" Rosemary asked, wrinkling up her nose.

"*Eat* you?" Gerty gasped, her bright, blue eyes as large as lakes.

All three exploded in laughter and howled until their sides ached. Dee-Dee darted about the room, adding to the ruckus. Tears streamed down Twiggedy's face as she helped Lissy to the table and sat her down.

"What is so funny about being killed and eaten like some helpless rabbit?" Lissy demanded, and the three howled again. Rosemary made bunny ears and wiggled them at Gerty, and Twiggedy hippity-hopped about like an oversized rabbit.

"I *do* hope you all are having a good time!" Lissy yelled over the din. The women were all choking now, fighting for air and holding their sides.

"Why did you get out a knife and shears then?" Lissy demanded stamping her foot, her hands on her hips. This started them to laughing again. They stamped their feet and paraded around with their hands on their hips.

"Girls, *girls! Enough!* The poor thing is frightened," Rose said, her dark eyes sparkling as she looked warmly at Lissy.

"Lissy," Twiggedy said calmly, "we were going to surprise you." Gerty giggled quietly.

"For your birthday, dear," Rose said softly.

"We were going to give you a haircut, and Gerty brought along a dress for you to try on so she could fit it to you," Twiggedy said.

"And I fashioned some moccasins for you," Rosemary said, pulling out a beautifully beaded pair of warm, fur-lined moccasins and laying them on the table.

Gerty uncovered her basket and pulled out a long, deep blue dress. No one had ever been so nice to her before.

"We were going to have a surprise party tonight, dear," Twiggedy said, "but the cat's out of the bag now." She walked over to the cabinet and pulled down a package wrapped in birch bark.

Lissy's hands trembled as she ever so gently opened the gift. Peeling back the layer of bark, she found a wooden book with leather hinges. She turned it over to find the front cover had the name "Elizabeth" carved into it. Next to that lay a small pouch. In the pouch was a tiny doll. It was carved with a sweet face and had a wisp of hair. The bright green eyes and tiny teeth smiled up at her. Lissy held it to her heart, tears flowing down her cheeks. To be loved was a wonderful thing.

All three ladies sniffled and snuffled. Rosemary got up to put the pot on to boil. Gerty straightened the table for lunch and Twiggedy busied herself, giving Lissy a moment of privacy. They bustled about the room, setting out platters of food. Gerty unwrapped strawberry tarts, herb-topped muffins and sweet, spicy pumpkin bread. Rose set out a tin of maple sugar candy and Twiggedy stirred the kettle of vegetable stew over the fire.

"I *jumped* out," Lissy said firmly over the room's din. She looked around to see the women's reaction to this announcement, but they merely carried on with their preparations.

"We know, dear," Twiggedy said casually. "Hand me those candles, Gerty."

"I jumped, because they *pushed* me," Lissy said, her voice louder.

"Yes, dear, we know," said Rosemary, dusting off the bench seats.

Lissy couldn't believe that the women weren't angry with her after her confession.

"Now come to your party, dear," Gerty said, smiling shyly. All three looked at Lissy, beaming at her. She looked at the feast laid out before her, without a mushroom in sight, and sighed with relief.

"Wait," Lissy said, coming to her senses. "My birthday is sometime in April. My mother couldn't remember if it was the sixth or seventh," she said, her voice trailing off into a whisper.

"Oh, *we* know, dear!" Twiggedy said, and the three women giggled.

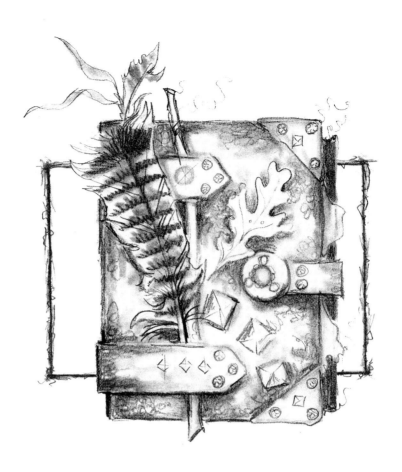

CHAPTER FOURTEEN –
The Calling of the Green

The next morning, blue jays flew through the forest calling one and all to gather and greet the sun. Melting snow hung from tree branches like brilliant crystals, catching the light and shooting rainbows about the woods.

"I don't understand what it is that you do," Lissy said to Twiggedy.

"Just watch and learn, child," Twiggedy said, as she and Gerty dragged her big cooking pot out into the snow. They set the heavy, blackened pot over the fire that Rose tended in the middle of the clearing. Rose went back into the tree house and came out with the large book that Twiggedy had stored in her cupboard.

Rose gently dusted off the leather cover, her eyes filling with tears. Gerty gently patted her shoulder. Twiggedy went inside and brought out a birch-bark canister, its lid decorated with little flying birds of brightly colored porcupine quills.

Dee-Dee arrived with her relatives, a flurry of chickadees that flitted from branch to branch. Perched high overhead in their dashing, sky-blue feathers, the blue jays loudly announced, *"Change! Change!"* Drumming woodpeckers and honking nuthatches appeared, as squirrels and deer stepped into the clearing. Lissy was awestruck, for she had never seen so many animals this close before.

"Ready, girls?" Twiggedy asked as she stirred the pot three times with a snake-like stick. Rose held the book, while Gerty held her basket and a white, birch-handled broom. Lissy wondered if she was going to fly on it over the treetops.

The three assumed their positions around the cooking pot over the fire. They joined hands and closed their eyes for a moment. A hush came over the forest. The animals stood motionless. The only sound Lissy heard was the thumping of her heart in her ears and the occasional sound of water dripping from the trees. Twiggedy looked up and winked at Lissy. Rose opened the book to a page marked with a striped turkey feather and held it in front of Twiggedy.

Then in a booming voice for all to hear, Twiggedy recited the story within:

"Long, long ago, it was once said,
That the bird song greened the trees—
In early spring at dusk and dawn
Their music tickled napping leaves.
Bird song in the woodland silent
Caused budding leaf to pop—
Opened the flower, fern and shrub,
From earthen floor to timber top!"

With that, Gerty pulled fragrant bergamot and goldenrod flowers dried last summer from her basket and tossed them into the steaming pot. Then Twiggedy opened the canister with the flying birds on it and poured a grayish-green powder into the cauldron.

"It is *done!* Out with the old and in with the new!" she cried, striking the pot with her stick.

The fire leaped high, throwing sparks as the pot belched a great cloud of smoke. The frightened animals scattered, and Lissy fell backwards into the slushy snow. Twiggedy and her friends giggled at the surprise, clapping their hands. Lissy stood up and watched the smoke spiral up through the treetops. Birds of every size and color had waited above in the canopy and flitted about in the smoke before they flew off.

Then all became quiet and serious again. Bog Rosemary tilted her head, listening to the wind song with a far off look in her eye. Twiggedy and Gerty watched her.

Tears rolled from her dark eyes and down her cheeks as she smiled and announced softly, "It worked. I hear them—they are coming."

All three witches were twirling about when Twiggedy grabbed Lissy's hand and pulled her into their circle. They sang and danced a jig around the pot.

Gerty sang:

"Sing a song of seasons,
Something bright in all,
Flowers in the summer,
Fires in the fall!"

Lissy nearly fell over—she knew these words from her Child's Garden of Verses book!

Twiggedy noticed the look of surprise on Lissy's face. "Those rhymes had to come from *somewhere*, didn't they, dear?" Twiggedy laughed and squeezed the girl's hand. The foursome frolicked about the woodland clearing like children. Lissy felt so loved and protected by these women that any thought of her family or sadness now seemed so far away.

CHAPTER FIFTEEN – The Journey

Lissy woke early the next day to the sound of the women whispering quietly by candlelight. Their hushed conversation sounded serious, unlike yesterday's jovial celebration. She knew something was wrong by the way they all looked at her, and Lissy's feeling of warmth and contentment evaporated.

Rose fiddled with a package on the table and dabbed the corners of her eyes, sniffling. Gerty played with the black lace about her throat and forced a polite grin. Twiggedy cleared her throat, and then broke the silence when she slammed her hands firmly on the table, making Dee-Dee leap from her perch.

"Child, we three have been discussing your situation. With the snows leaving, you may be the target of Shadow Chaser again. It's not safe for you here. I know we put a protective spell on you to keep you safe, but it's only a matter of time before Shadow Chaser finds you."

Lissy's heart dropped like a stone in a well at this announcement. She had almost forgotten the danger that she had been in.

"We feel it best that you travel back with the girls to Bog Rosemary's home. You'll be safer there," Twiggedy said, looking away.

Lissy was speechless and looked into their faces. Rose slid the package that she had been fiddling with over to the teary-eyed girl.

"I made this for you," Rose said, her dark eyes looking deeply into Lissy's. Lissy unwrapped the cloth to find a leather necklace with a small pouch attached. She pulled out two tiny clay tablets with marks inscribed on them. One had a three-tined fork and the other had a strange, angular "S" shape. "These are ancient runes," Rose explained. "They are signs of great protection and power as you begin your journey with us." She tied the necklace around Lissy's slender neck.

Lissy placed the runes back into the pouch and pulled the string to shut it tightly. She glanced at Twiggedy, but Twiggedy stood up and looked away. She had already packed Lissy's things and she went to get them from the cupboard. Lissy couldn't believe that they all had decided her fate without even asking her. Everything, including her pink dress, was contained in the parcel. Twiggedy must have grown tired of her like her own family had and wanted her to leave, too. She must have done something to upset the old woman; otherwise she could have stayed here with her protective necklace.

Lissy took a deep breath and picked up the bundle, but she would not look at Twiggedy.

"It won't take me long to get ready," she said coolly. The three women were quiet and studied the contents of their teacups.

"You'll understand one day," Rose said stirring her tea.

When everyone had finished their breakfast and packed, Twiggedy opened the door for them to go. They had to leave at first light—they had long journey ahead. Lissy pulled her coat on, only two sizes too large now. She wore her cozy, new moccasins and warm, blue dress.

Taking her bundle and tucking it under her arm, she stepped outside into the pink morning light. Dee-Dee came to sit on her shoulder and cocked her little black-capped head at her and tears formed in Lissy's eyes. The bird fluttered off into the woods. Gerty and Rose took a deep breath and eyed each other as Twiggedy reached for Lissy's shoulder to say goodbye. Lissy just shrugged it off and looked away.

Gerty and Rose stepped out into the early morning light. No sooner had they crossed the threshold than they each changed form. Gerty Goodapple shape-shifted into the opossum that Lissy had seen waddling about the woods on the day of her arrival, and Bog Rosemary became a silvery-brown beaver. Lissy's mouth dropped open. They came to stand at her side.

"This is how we travel, dear. To blend in with the world, we must wear a mask," explained Twiggedy as she bid the group farewell. The three trod through the snow with Gerty leading the way and slow-moving Rose in the rear. Lissy didn't dare look back—her chest filled with hurt and bitterness and felt as if it would explode. She was angry with Twiggedy for making her leave.

They had walked for a long while when Rose finally spoke. "It is a brave thing she is doing, child, for the Shadow Chaser will go there *first.*"

Lissy startled at the words. They sounded odd coming from Rose's lumbering beaver form. It was then that she finally understood and she turned around to look back at the little tree house and to call for Twiggedy, but the forest had closed in around them like a gray blanket of shadow and dread. As she turned back to follow the others into the woods, she felt a giant claw of panic grab her stomach.

CHAPTER SIXTEEN – Beaver Isle

The little group had traveled for the better part of the day and still had far to go. They stopped to rest. The journey was hard on Rose. She was not used to traveling so far on land. When they stopped to nibble on the biscuits Twiggedy had packed, Lissy finally spoke.

"Where are we going, anyway?" she asked, feeling awkward speaking to their animal selves.

"My lodge is on Beaver Isle, in the middle of Cedar Lake," Rose answered, her dark, beady eyes glistening at the mention of home.

"And I live in the old orchard not far from there," Gerty added, cleaning her long, pink rat-like tail.

Lissy thought what a picture this would make if anyone saw them—a little girl sitting on a log, casually chatting with a beaver and an opossum!

"So, what is it that you do, Rose?" Lissy asked trying not to notice the beaver's yellow teeth and runny nose.

"I am the seer of the lake. I look into the future, carve runes, and do my writings to preserve the past," Rose said.

"What about you, Gerty?" Lissy asked politely, not believing this ungainly, unsightly creature could be the prim and proper woman she had come to know.

"Me? Oh, well, I deliver dreams," the opossum answered, drooling and grinning shyly.

"Oh, Gerty, you make the finest dreams around! She is much too modest, really," chattered Rose. "She paints them on sheets of silken web and delivers them each night to sleeping children," Rose giggled delightedly.

"Stop, now, Rose, you're embarrassing me! I just love what I do," Gerty clucked, her pink nose blushing pinker. "Anyway ladies, we need to continue, we don't want to be caught in these woods after dark."

Lissy listened to the spinsterish fuss and banter between her two companions. By the time they had readied to leave, she had grown accustomed to their furry forms. The sun was already making its own journey westward and the air grew cooler as they continued through blue-violet shadows. Squirrels ran ahead and Lissy noticed a chickadee perched nearby. She wondered if it might be Dee-Dee but since Dee-Dee looked just like all the others in her family, it would be pretty hard to tell.

As they continued on their way, Lissy noticed changes in the forest. No longer were there the toppled poplar trees, nor beech or maple. She smelled the aroma of spicy cedars, and apparently the others had, too.

"We're getting closer to home now!" Rose announced, clicking her teeth in excitement.

The group worked their way to the shoreline through the pungent smelling trees and shrubby, red dogwoods.

"There it is," Rose said. She held out a paw and pointed toward a small island. The frozen lake, surrounded by dark cedars, was so beautiful it took Lissy's breath away. No wonder Rose was anxious to get home! Her pace quickened and Lissy had to run to keep up. By now the sun was ready to settle in for the night and it seemed to be in just as much of a hurry as they were. The wind blew dancing "snow-snakes" across the ice and the only sound was the crunching of the traveler's ten feet through the snow.

They reached the island and rested, collapsing onto the bank, panting and laughing. Lissy lay back in the snow and looked up into the sky. She was lost in her thoughts of spring with its flowers and warmth when Rose towered over her in her familiar brown cloak.

Lissy sat up in surprise and saw Gerty brushing off her gray shawl and adjusting her wide-brimmed straw hat. For a moment, Lissy envied these wonderful women and their magical ways. She got up to go into Rose's home. Lissy was amazed at the sight of the modified beaver lodge tucked in among the trees along the southern shore.

"I'll get a fire started," Rose said, opening the door as Gerty stamped the snow off her black boots.

Lissy stepped inside and looked around at the dark interior. There were no windows, but the lodge was nice and roomy, unlike like Twiggedy's cramped maple tree house. Rose lit one candle and then another. Tools and clay lay strewn across the table as if she had just stepped away from her work for a cup of tea. A thick, red wool blanket was folded on the bed. Books were stacked in piles and stuck in every nook and cranny. Gerty went about tidying and dusting shelves with her hand.

"Leave it be, Gerty," Rose said quietly. "Come have some mint tea."

Lissy peeled off her coat and Rose hung it by the fire, then left the room through dark green curtains. Lissy was curious and went to see where she had gone. To her surprise, Rose didn't have an upstairs like Twiggedy, but a downstairs. Rose came up carrying small, frozen parcels.

"Dinner," she said to Lissy, grinning while she unwrapped them and placed them into the glowing coals.

"Mud pies?" Lissy asked confused, as she studied a long, clay-packed shape. But Rose just giggled like a little girl with a secret and joined Gerty for tea by the fire.

"Where shall I put my things?" asked Lissy, looking about curiously. Rose pointed to a loft in the corner over her own bed. Lissy found a ladder nearby and climbed up.

The upper part of the lodge, warmed by the fire, was cozy and inviting, and Lissy suddenly felt very sleepy. She set her bundle down and plopped onto the soft furs and deep feather mattress. The bed enveloped her like a baby in its mother's arms, and Lissy felt warm, comfortable, and safe. She tried to get up to go to tea, but the bed pulled her into its depths and she was soon fast asleep.

Lissy woke to the smell of something delicious wafting up to the loft. She rubbed her eyes, forgetting where she was for a moment. She crawled her way out of the mountainous bed and climbed down the ladder. Gerty and Rose smiled at her as she came to the table.

"Just in time for dinner," Rose giggled, as she pulled the sizzling parcels from the coals and placed them on a wooden platter. The three stared at the steaming clay cakes, their mouths watering.

"I wouldn't have thought that mud would smell so good," Lissy said hungrily. Gerty and Rose laughed at her. Rose carefully put a pie on each plate, then reached over and cracked Lissy's open. A cloud of steam billowed out and brought with it the smell of freshly baked seasoned trout. Lissy picked up a piece of the flaky, white meat, blew on it, and popped it into her mouth.

"Mud pies are divine!" she exclaimed.

"They are indeed," Gerty said as she opened hers. The three ate their dinner in silence. It seemed strange that Twiggedy wasn't there to join them. A sudden gust of wind outside whistled and whined through the door. Rose hurried to the door and opened it. She sniffed the air and looked out, scanning the lake. The sun was setting a fiery orange in the purple sky.

"Trouble in the air," she said, sounding concerned, and that distant look passed over her face again. She placed her hand over her heart and whispered, *"Take care old friend."*

Then a familiar sound sent a chill down Lissy's spine. The howling yip of coyotes broke the stillness of the evening, echoing eerily from somewhere deep in the heart of Twiggedy's Popple-Pine Forest.

CHAPTER SEVENTEEN – Shadows

After the girls had left, Twiggedy went around tidying up her tiny tree house. When she opened the door to sweep out the dust, Dee-Dee flew up and landed on her shoulder. The tiny bird whispered in her ear.

"I feel it too, Dee-Dee…something's not right," said Twiggedy, as a gust of wind whipped around her like a coiled snake. The trees stirred in their sleep. She hoped that the three made it back to Rose's place safely.

The sun had just slipped past the hushed forest toward the horizon, taking with it the last of the golden light, when she heard the all too familiar sound of coyotes.

Their strange music rose and fell as it was carried on the wind through the shuddering trees.

"Hmm," she said to Dee-Dee, "we must be on our guard with those sly dogs about." Her sharp eyes studied the shadows before she shut the door.

The next morning Twiggedy-Jig woke with a start and she quickly got up to look out the window. During the night, the air had warmed and a mist now shrouded her forest home. She stepped out into the slushy snow to listen. In the thick fog, everything was gray and silent except for the occasional tree that moaned as if having a nightmare. She pulled her shawl tighter around her.

"Oh, this is not good, this feeling I have," she said as Dee-Dee flitted about like a bouncing ball. With a few more steps, Twiggedy knew why she felt this way. Tracks in the snow, made during the night, were now distorted from the early morning thaw. Whoever had made the tracks was sure to be lurking nearby, waiting for her. Branches clattered and limbs chattered in the wind.

Suddenly a maple tossed a twig into her path, warning her of danger. "Thank you, Mother Maple," Twiggedy said to the tree as she pulled her black shawl over her head and, changing into the Pileated woodpecker that Lissy had once seen, flew to the nearest poplar. Her long, strong tail feathers held her close to the trunk as she leaned out, her yellow eyes peering into the mist. She was spiraling higher up the tree when she first heard the faint steps of an animal moving carefully through the wood. She couldn't be sure if it was friend or foe, as the stealthy step of the hunter and the hunted sound alike.

But then she saw the hint of a dark, ghost-like form slithering fluidly in and out among the trees. She was climbing higher still when she heard the panting of the creature from somewhere below. A movement to her right startled her, and she turned just in time to see gaping black jaws and white fangs snap at her. It had grabbed a mouthful of her feathers!

Her red crest rose and she uttered a cry of alarm. Up the tree trunk she hopped, holding her damaged wing against her body, until she was out of reach of the hunter, coyote. She never had any problems with the coyotes before, as they ordinarily kept to themselves.

"My land and my stars, you gave me a fright!" Twiggedy said shaking, scolding the beast. "What are you doing in my wood?"

"It's the child I am after. Where are you hiding her, Twiggedy-Jig?" Coyote snarled.

"Why are you after a child? Aren't there enough mice and rabbits in the field for you to chase?" Twiggedy pretended not to know what he was talking about and hopped a little higher up the tree trunk.

"Why don't you come down and we'll talk about it," Coyote snickered. "Just how long can you stay up there, anyway? Take me to the girl and I will spare your life."

"Now, what on earth are you going to do with a child? They are too sweet for your likes. You seem to enjoy dead things left to rot in the woods," Twiggedy said, trying to get more information.

"Actually, I don't want her, but *Shadow Chaser does,*" laughed Coyote, "and she *always* gets what she wants."

Twiggedy was now truly frightened for Lissy. If Shadow Chaser was sending others to do her dirty work, then no one could be trusted. She had to warn the girls.

"So why doesn't Shadow Chaser come herself?" Twiggedy argued, stalling for a plan.

"Shadow Chaser lives beyond the lake and has offered me many things in return for the child," the coyote yipped, wagging his tail anxiously.

Twiggedy had to do something, and fast. With her wing damaged, she was forced to half-hop and half-flap, as she moved from one tree to the next. Coyote ran after her.

"You can't get away that easily," he drooled.

Twiggedy hopped and flapped from tree to tree, with the coyote on her tail the whole way. Exhausted, she clutched the bark with her strong nails and rested. Coyote sat patiently below her, his tongue lolling.

"I can play this game as long as you like, you old wood hen," he shouted, pacing nervously.

Twiggedy waited. Dee-Dee landed next to her on the branch. Twiggedy told her old friend to find Rose and tell her of the danger. As Twiggedy watched the little bird fly away, the sun rose higher in the sky and the fog began to burn off.

Twiggedy had an idea. She hopped to the nearest tree and flapped to the next. On she went into the heart of the Popple-Pine forest with Coyote following her. The further she went into the woods, the deeper the snow became, forcing him to lift his legs higher with each step. This little game went on for the better part of the day. Coyote, his tongue lolling and his steps becoming slower, finally collapsed in exhaustion and watched her from below.

After a while, the wind started picking up and the trees swayed, whispering to Twiggedy. *Perfect,* she thought, *if everything works right, I'll soon be on my way.*

It was almost time to put her plan into action. The sun disappeared and the forest air became much cooler. She waited patiently.

Finally, in the pale, orange glow of twilight, she flapped her damaged wing as if falling and slid down the trunk within reach of her resting enemy. This instantly snapped Coyote to attention. His eyes shone like amber glass as he lunged at the trunk of the tree.

Twiggedy timed it just right and jumped at the last second. Coyote's jaws snapped, but he clamped down on nothing but icy air. Coyote yipped as he broke through the crust and it bit into his flesh. The temperature had been dropping steadily and the once slushy snow had now formed a thin, crusty layer of ice on top.

Twiggedy began making her way out of the heart of the forest. She stopped to look over her velvety, black-feathered shoulder. There was Coyote, drooling and wheezing, trying to keep up the chase. But each step he took ended in bloody gashes and him yowling in pain as ice sliced through his fur.

"Foolish dog," Twiggedy clucked. She, too, was tiring from the day's events. In the dying light she spied a silver beech tree about ten yards away with an oval opening half way up the trunk. She flapped as hard as she could to reach it.

In a wild fury, Coyote leaped up to follow her, leaving a blood-spattered trail. He took a final lunge at her as she grabbed a toehold on the smooth barked tree.

Twiggedy threw herself inside the opening. Tumbling safely into a pile of leaves, she collapsed, her heart racing.

Outside in the cold blackness, the bleeding coyote howled. He was angry but would not give up that easily.

Twiggedy could only hope that Dee-Dee reached Rose's lodge to warn them. Burrowing into the leaves, she wrapped her torn shawl around her, curled up and went to sleep.

CHAPTER EIGHTEEN – Foolish Coyote

The next morning, a beautiful pink and blue patchwork quilt of clouds spread out over the Popple-Pine forest. Twiggedy peered out from the hole to find Coyote gone, and no tracks indicating which way he had gone. Sometime during the night, the icy crust had become solid enough for him to walk on without breaking through. *Oh, this was not good.* Twiggedy had to get to the others. Since she wouldn't be able to fly to warn them, she had but one choice to travel safely. Smoothing her skirt and squeezing herself through the oval knothole, she changed into a porcupine.

She climbed down quietly, her thirty-thousand quills clattering softly with each step. Last night's escape from Coyote was too close for comfort. She had to move quickly and silently now. She suspected that Coyote had not gone far and walked carefully back towards her home.

With her mind on her long journey, she broke into a trot, but her short legs would not carry her as quickly as she would have liked. She was almost home when a blue jay called loudly and several chickadees darted past her in a panic. She heard the wheezing and panting of the injured beast behind her and turned to look. She whirled about, staring into the twisted, sneering face of Coyote.

"You again, Coyote? You want more games to play today?" Twiggedy backed up as the animal crept nearer, his cold, yellow-green eyes narrowing into slits. She shuffled side-to-side, rattling her quills.

"No beast, however foolish, would *dare* to mess with my arsenal of barbed quills, Coyote," she said defiantly, as he got so close that she felt his hot breath on her face. "Maybe you would like to be the first!" And with that she grunted a warning and backed up to a maple.

"Not a step closer, you mangy dog! I am not the feeble old woman you think I am," Twiggedy declared loudly. Coyote stopped for a moment, which was all she needed to scramble up the backside of the tree. Coyote sprang at her, his mouth open wide. She swatted him heavily, full in the face with her armored tail, knocking him off his feet in a burst of pain and rage.

Coyote wailed in agony, his muzzle full of needle-sharp quills. The thick, brown and white tail quills hung from his nose like a painful moustache and dangled from under his eyes and black lips.

"Ow-ooh, what a fool I am for listening to Shadow Chaser," he cried through contorted lips, "and even more of a fool for not listening to you, Twiggedy-Jig!"

Twiggedy scooted higher up the tree to get safely out of his way. She watched as he rolled and batted at the quills. In a way, she felt bad for the pitiful beast.

"So, you are the first to tangle with me, Coyote," she said, carefully backing down the tree to inspect his wounds. "Stop moving so much, they'll just go in deeper."

"Deeper?" he yelped, pawing at the quills poking out from his nose.

"The more you mess with them, the deeper they will drive into your flesh, making them much more difficult to pull out," Twiggedy said.

Coyote lay still, panting and slobbering, his badly cut legs bleeding again. Quills stuck out every which way from his swollen face. Twiggedy stepped closer and he winced, trying to pull away from her.

"Be *still*, Coyote, I'm going to help you, for I am as foolish as you." With that being said, Twiggedy changed back into her old witch woman form and approached Coyote. His swollen eyes grew wild with fear at the sight of a human and he fainted.

"Good thing," she muttered, "because this won't be pretty." Twiggedy pulled out her bag and found the dried yarrow and red clover flowers needed to clean his wounds, and some fuzzy, dried mullein leaves to cover them. She prepared an aspen bark tea for him to drink when he woke, but by that time, she would be far from this place.

"You are what you are Coyote, it's your nature and I'll never trust you," Twiggedy said, clucking her tongue at the pitiful creature resting in the place she had cleared for him.

Twiggedy, you old fool, she chuckled softly, shaking her head, *you could have just left the beast here to suffer, but it's your nature not to.*

The evening sky, painted turquoise, yellow, and orange, smiled down on her as she left her Popple-Pine wood in search of the others.

CHAPTER NINETEEN – Spring's Return

Days went by and balmy weather woke the trees, giving the forest world a taste of the spring days to come. Lying in bed at night, Lissy imagined great clouds of birds coming from the south, carrying with them the sun's warmth. She hoped that they would arrive soon.

She fingered the dried herbs in the pouch around her neck. Gerty had given her some stinging nettle and yarrow herbs to add to the protection when the howling at night had begun. But the coyotes had stopped, and everyone was even more worried about Twiggedy.

Lissy became restless and would unpack her toys and try to play. She'd open her book and feel the carved name on the cover, hug the little doll, and then wrap them up again.

After dinner, she would go out on the front porch and listen for the return of the birds that Rose had talked about. On those purple and pink candy-striped evenings, as the sun slid into the cedars on the other side of the lake, she would sit and think about her family. She wondered if anyone ever cried about her, or if maybe they celebrated her mysterious disappearance. She tried to think back to the day at her uncle's cabin on the lake when it all started. She would start to remember, but would then be distracted by one thing or another.

Rose was hard at work in the evenings, her lamp often burning long into the night as she molded and worked her clay. Lissy missed the comforting ticking of Twiggedy's strange clock and the sound of Dee-Dee settling for the night. Gerty missed her home, and began acting more nervous, often voicing that she should really be on her way to start her spring-cleaning.

The next morning, Lissy sat up in bed and listened to a weird noise that sounded like a squeaky, rusty wagon-wheel going around. Rose walked to the door and opened it. A gust of warm air burst into the room. Lissy jumped up and raced down from the loft. She heard the sound again, a constant whirring.

"A beating of wings cutting the air…" Rose whispered, looking glassy-eyed as her voice trailed off.

"…thousands and thousands," Lissy finished. They both squinted into the sky. Not a moment later, they heard a sound in the distance like the cheering of a crowd. A sweeping, black cloud turned and separated, and birds seemed to tumble down from the sky. They swung from every branch and cattail, flashing their scarlet-red shoulder patches like generals of a feathered-army setting up camp.

"Conquer-ing! Conquer-ing!" cried the red-winged blackbirds at their posts.

Lissy covered her ears and ran outside to greet them. She went to the shore and looked out over the lake. The ice had thawed overnight, separating the island from the forest. Lissy ran along the water's edge and yelled to the birds flying overhead, "Thank you for bringing spring home!"

When Lissy got back to the lodge, she found Gerty and Rose talking quietly. Since the ice had thawed, Lissy was safe and Gerty would be going—she didn't like being away from home that long. Rose understood, but for Lissy, the excitement of the day had melted like the ice and everything became quiet and gray. One by one, everyone was leaving her, and that night Lissy cried herself to sleep.

CHAPTER TWENTY – The Dream

That night Lissy dreamed that her shadow called out to her from behind what seemed to be a wall of dancing mist. Lissy tried to reach out to it and pull it to safety, but could not. When she woke the next morning, she went to the door to watch the sun come up over Cedar Lake. The mist danced over the water, as it had in her dream, but no shadow was there to greet her. Sometime during the night, Gerty had left without a sound.

Each day Lissy heard a new arrival on the lake. There were flocks of geese and mergansers bobbing about on the water. She and Rose would sit and listen to clouds of cranes trumpeting their musical "ka-rroo" and the nightly yodel of handsomely dressed loons. They watched orange-breasted robins flash through the woods each day, and listened to the sounds of peepers and chorus frogs singing at night. Lissy longed to be in the woods to see the squirrels at play, and the deer frolicking and celebrating fresh green things to eat. Velvet-brown mourning cloak butterflies danced over the tight-fisted fern heads and the pink-and-white striped spring beauty wildflowers. Lissy watched the forest around the lake becoming more and more green with the magic of the sun's golden touch.

Each night in her dreams, her shadow called to her, becoming clearer and stronger. At times it seemed so clear, that she felt she could reach out and grab the outstretched hand and finally have her shadow back.

Rose had started teaching Lissy the runic alphabet to keep her busy. Lissy had always enjoyed school back home and could read well, but she found this schooling much more entertaining. Rose showed her the plants, birds, and animal life of the lake. Lissy enjoyed this time together.

One night, the two of them watched a spring storm roll in across the lake. The wind whipped their hair and the cold, black waves became tipped in frothy white, reminding Lissy of the white cats. The two hurried inside.

"Have you seen the white cats, Rose?" Lissy asked. "My mother told me once that they can grab people and pull them under the water when they weren't looking. But Bob just laughed at me—he said they weren't real."

"Anything can grab you if you aren't looking," Rose said, quietly shutting the door. "You can be sure that when there's a change in the weather, something is going to happen."

As the wind picked up, it howled and whistled through the cracks in the door so loudly that they did not hear the tiny chickadee tapping outside. Dee-Dee huddled underneath some twigs and branches in the corner to wait out the storm.

Rose tucked Lissy into bed as the storm raged over Beaver Isle. She felt safe and warm in the strong wooden lodge, and soon fell asleep to the sounds of Rose working at her table below.

That night Lissy dreamed of her shadow again. It danced in the mist to the eerie yet pleasant song that the cedars sang. For the first time, things became clear. Lissy saw that her shadow wore a white bone necklace and a long, shimmering blue-black dress studded in star-like crystals. It hovered in the mist, holding out a rose-pink shawl for Lissy to take.

"Clothe yourself in brightness," the shadow woman told her. Lissy reached out for the stunning shawl and saw the shadow dive into the water, crying like a loon.

"Wait, come back!" Lissy cried. She sat up in bed. Everything was dark and quiet in the lodge except for Rose's gentle snoring. The storm had moved on, and now drops from the trees pattered the roof. Then she heard it—not once, but twice. Lissy felt a tug in her stomach and knew she wasn't dreaming, that she was wide-awake. It was the cry of the loon—her shadow was calling her!

She got out of bed and dressed quietly in the dark. Grabbing her coat and shoes, she crept outside and put them on there, so as not to wake Rose. The lake was covered in a thick blanket of mist, just like in her dream, and the waves lapped hypnotically at the shore. The loon called again as if reminding her that it was still there. The predawn light brightened enough for her to see her way to the water's edge.

Stepping between two birch trees like a gateway into another world, Lissy heard the loon call again. The fog was so thick that she couldn't tell where the shore ended and the water started. She looked for the mysterious bird, but could only hear it, dipping and diving, gently breaking the water. The mists enveloped her, and then she saw it.

The loon flipped crystal water droplets into the air and stretched her wings out elegantly. Lissy was frantic to get out into the water, but she wasn't a very good swimmer, and besides, the water was too cold. She stuck her hands in her pockets to warm them. Something tickled her chilled fingers. She pulled out the little plastic canoe with the chip in its side.

Cradling it in both hands and closing her eyes, she wished as mightily as she could. She opened her eyes, but nothing seemed to have happened.

"Stupid magic," she muttered, "nothing ever comes from wishing." She was so angry she was about to toss it into the lake, but she changed her mind. Something caught her eye. A flash of color peeked out from behind some cattails. Lissy ran over and pulled back the brown reeds and grasses, uncovering a battered, red canoe. Rolling it over, she found the smooth, wooden paddle and pulled the boat to the water. She had been in her uncle's canoe with her father before, and remembered to crawl in so

as not to tip it. She steadied herself and then shoved off
with all her might.

Nervously, she paddled out into the deep water. She
dared not look over the side for fear of looking into the
eyes of the fierce, white cat. Then the loon appeared out
of the steely-black water and paused, waiting for her.
The fog began to thin and pink clouds stretched over the
water like a giant hand, reassuring her. Lissy paddled
nearer to where the loon bobbed. Gracefully, it tucked
its head into its star-studded black feathers and mewed
softly to her. The ruby-red eye stared at her, unblinking,
as it began to swim slowly across the lake.

Lissy, caught up in the moment and so taken with
the loon's beauty, followed the loon through the mist
without a thought.

Bog Rosemary woke to the calls of the loon on the
lake. She stretched and climbed out of bed throwing on
her cloak to go out and inspect the lodge for damage
from the night's storm. But, when she opened the door,
in tumbled the wet, miserable chickadee.

"Dee-Dee!" Rose exclaimed at the sight of the
bedraggled bird. She picked her up and carried her to the
fire. The little bird was almost lifeless. Rose wrapped her
up in a warm cloth until the little bird felt stronger. After
a few moments, Dee-Dee started chirping and fluttering
about the table.

"Is Lissy in danger?" Rose gasped, and ran to the
door. The fog blanket still lay on the lake. "Where on

earth could she have gone?" She ran to the shore and found the old canoe in the grass by the dock missing.

"Oh, girls, there's trouble now," Rose said to herself as she looked out across the lake. She could barely make out a form out on the water, heading toward Pine Rock Island.

"Did you get my message?" said a voice in the fog.

Rose whirled around to find Gerty and Twiggedy hurrying down the path from her lodge.

"Come on ladies, I hope that we are in time," said Rose, pointing to the small canoe headed straight for the home of Shadow Chaser.

CHAPTER TWENTY-ONE –
Shadow Chaser

Lissy paddled after the loon, following it until another island loomed before her. It was rocky and rugged, covered with windswept pines and spruce. The sun came up over the trees, painting everything in golden light. The water was shallow here, which made Lissy feel better. The lapping waves rocked the little boat, its bottom thumping dully against the rocks. The loon swam toward the island, turning around and eyeing Lissy for a moment before disappearing beneath the water.

Lissy could smell the pine scent wafting from the island, drawing her closer. She paddled as close to shore as she could, pulled the canoe up onto the rocky beach and placed the paddle inside. The thinning fog lifted and sent twisting, turning shapes dancing across the water, and she stopped to watch them. A sudden burst of birds taking flight brought Lissy to her senses.

She left the shore and stepped into the silence of the pines. The bed of soft, rusty-brown needles formed a trail, and she could smell smoke. The trail led to a small lodge standing in a clearing. To her surprise, it was shaped much like Rose's—it was round and dome-shaped, but was covered with fresh smelling spruce boughs. Smoke curled from the central hole in the top, and there was a ragged, tanned deerskin with strange markings covering the door. Lissy tiptoed closer.

She looked up into an overhanging pine tree and saw a small, grayish-owl wink one yellow eye at her. It ruffled up its feathered collar and stared at her.

"Hello?" Lissy half-whispered, afraid of who or what would come out of the strange lodge.

She gathered up her courage and peeked inside, pulling back the heavy hide. She crept into the darkness and the hide dropped back into place behind her. The blackness seemed to swallow all light and sound, along with Lissy. She became dizzy and felt as if she were swirling around in nothingness, but when her eyes adjusted, she saw coals as red as the loon's eyes glowing in a fire pit.

The room had a musty odor about it. There were bundles of herbs hanging here and there, and she jumped when something brushed against her head. Afraid she might trip, she crawled on her hands and knees and felt her way to the fire. She found a supply of wood nearby, and tossed some birch bark and sticks onto the coals.

The fire caught immediately, devouring the pieces she had thrown in, and flames shot up, lighting the inside of the lodge. Lissy's mouth dropped open. Suspended from the ceiling were a hundred or more necklaces, some of crystal and others of pearl. They caught the light and shot tiny rainbows around the lodge. She had reached out to touch one when she heard a noise outside. She froze, trying not to breathe. The fire crackled and spit. Straightening up from her crouch, she knocked into some of the jewels, sending them swinging and clink-ing. Suddenly things became too quiet, inside and out. The fire had started to die down and Lissy couldn't tell which way led to the door. She saw a gray shadow drift silently across the room.

She held her breath again and started feeling very sick. This must be the home of Shadow Chaser. She reached for the rune pouch around her neck and, to her horror, realized it wasn't there.

"Now you've really done it, stupid," she said quietly to herself, then clapped her hand over her mouth, her heart in her throat. Outside on the lake, geese began splashing and honking. Something must have startled them. She added more branches to the fire to give her enough light to get back to the door. Through the maze of necklaces she went, until something swinging gently off to her right caught her eye, and she stopped—it seemed so familiar.

"It's real?" she gasped. She reached out to touch the shimmering crystal that Shadow Chaser had taken from her jewelry box. In the glow of firelight, it was even more beautiful than she remembered from her dream, and the stone seemed to be singing the song of the cedars, calling to her. She reached out and plucked the necklace from where it hung. The moment she touched it, a feeling like a jolt of electricity shot through her and she knew for certain that it belonged to her.

Without another minute to lose, she quickly put it around her neck and pulled back the hide. The air outside was cold and damp, and blue-gray clouds passed before the sun. She peeked out the door and saw the pines swinging and moving. They were singing to her again! She remembered their song that first night in the forest, when Twiggedy came to rescue her. And they were warning her now.

Lissy crept out the door and was walking toward the place she'd left the canoe, when she heard a twig snap behind her.

CHAPTER TWENTY-TWO –
The Encounter

I must get to the canoe—now, she said to herself, tugging at her necklace. *Don't turn around.*

Rose's words rang in her mind: "Anything can get you if you are not looking."

But right now, I really don't want to look, she argued with herself. Then Lissy heard the hoarse, throaty cry of a disgruntled heron. She watched the bird glide across the water and land in the shallows near the canoe. There was something about the bird's golden-eyed squint that reminded her of Rose. How she longed for her friends right now!

Lissy whirled around and came face to face with a wicked, hungry looking silver-white lynx. A white cat! Lissy's scream caught in her throat. The eyes of the beast glowed like cold metal, and its pale fur gleamed.

Its paws were as big as skillets, and it padded quietly around her. She knew in her heart this must be Shadow Chaser. Lissy felt the necklace about her neck, and the giant cat, its mouth filled with razor-sharp teeth, screamed with rage. Lissy's body shook and she was sure her legs were going to collapse under her. She couldn't move. If she ran, the white cat would be upon her.

The cat edged closer to her, enjoying her panic and fright. It grinned viscously, changing slowly into the Indian woman from her dream.

"Sssso, you've found the necklaccce," she hissed at Lissy. The woman's eyes were cold and without emotion. Her silver-gray hair was pulled back tightly into a bun and she wore the net-like, black shawl that Lissy remembered from her dream.

"You know it belongs to me, Lisssy," the woman spat at her. "You didn't want it, so I took it for my collection."

"How do you know my name?" Lissy asked, backing up slowly toward the lake.

"Oh child, quite easssssy. I have been watching you for a long, long time," the wicked woman laughed. "Much longer than you know, my dear."

"Mother says to watch out for the white cats, Bob!" the woman imitated Lissy's voice. Lissy's eyes grew wide and she caught her breath.

"Yes, dear, who do you think put the bait out for you on the shore. I watched you all that time from my perch. I saw Bob knock you down, I saw you pick up the canoe. But best of all, I heard your wish," and she howled with fiendish laughter. "Why, here it is."

102

Shadow Chaser produced the golden leaf that had fallen from the tree that day and mocked, *"Fits like a glove!"* She smiled cruelly, her eyes narrowing into slits. *"I wish I could be here always, I don't want to go back home,"* again imitating Lissy. She held the leaf to her heart and batted her eyelashes like an actress.

"Well, you got your wish, dear, are you happy?" Shadow Chaser asked, crumpling the leaf in her hand. "From now on, you will live here with me and be my very own toy, my slave, forever! You shall never return to your home—never!"

Tears welled in Lissy's eyes, but she bit her lip. "First, you were abandoned by your family," growled Shadow Chaser, "and then by Twiggedy Jig. Gerty Goodapple left you too, and now not even Bog Rosemary has come to your rescue!" Lissy felt completely empty and alone, and despair began to fill her.

"That's right, dear, I'm the only one who cares about you. What about your little friends, Lissssy, where are they? If they cared about you, wouldn't they be here to help you? Because you are much too stupid to ever find your own way." Then the woman continued in a kinder, lilting voice, "Besides, you need me. Why, I have been with you all along like a true friend, always at your heels, always just behind you. Like a shadow, you might say." Shadow Chaser threw back her head and laughed at the pitiful situation the girl had gotten herself into.

Lissy was angry with everyone. She fumed inside, her emptiness turning to rage, and she started to shake.

"My name is not Lissy, it's Elizabeth!" she screamed, her face bright red.

The woman jumped back at the girl's outburst, as if Lissy had punched her hard in the stomach.

"And my Grandma loves me, and my aunts and my uncle!" she screamed. Her voice echoed across the lake much like the call of the loon had. Lissy managed a smile as her voice bounced off the water. She heard the howl of a coyote hiding among the spruce shadows on shore.

The woman was enraged, her white knuckles clenched in huge fists. She immediately became the white cat again, the silver-whiskered lynx with the pale, gray eyes.

The sun came out from behind the clouds and as Lissy backed toward the rocky shore, she saw it in front of her. Her very own shadow—her shadow, in its long, blue dress, much taller than she, and with longer hair. For an instant she was delighted, but then looked up into the blazing eyes of the lynx as it readied to pounce on her.

The cat saw the girl's shadow and screamed, its hot breath scalding Lissy's face. It cringed and stepped back. Lissy heard splashing sounds coming toward shore, then saw a ghostly gray shape race through the pine trees, panting. It exploded into the clearing, knocking Lissy over.

But the coyote didn't attack Lissy—it went after the cat! The cat hissed and leaped, scrambling for a tree limb, but the branch cracked under its weight, sending the lynx back to the ground with a thump. Coyote snapped its wounded jaws at the cornered cat. The lynx swiped at the coyote with its long, razor-sharp claws, its eyes alive with fire.

104

"You want to fight, Coyote?" spat the wild cat. "After all I promised you, thisss is how you repay me?" The cat was ready to pounce on the once-beaten coyote, when out of the pines loped two other coyotes. The three surrounded the snarling, crouching beast, and the angry cat, its pale eyes wild, sensed a losing battle and turned tail to run.

Off she sprang, hopping from rock to rock, across the shallows of the lake, slipping and sliding. All three coyotes went after her like a gray streak. The cat scrambled through the shallows and into the spruce forest behind the small island. When she reached the forest all three coyotes were hot on her trail yipping with the thrill of the chase.

Slowly, Lissy stood up. She wiped off her dress and looked up to see Twiggedy, Gerty, and Rose stepping out of the trees. Lissy ran to hug Twiggedy.

"I found my shadow," she beamed. "See, I told you it was taller than me!" Lissy said, then stopped. "Why didn't you help me?" she scowled at the three.

"You had to do it all yourself, child," Twiggedy said quietly.

"But we were nearby," Rose said and winked at her. Then Lissy remembered the heron and the owl.

"That was you standing in the water and Gerty up in the pine." Lissy brightened.

"Yes, dear, we were here to watch over you," Gerty grinned shyly.

"We've always watched over you," Rose said dabbing at her dark eyes.

"But, the coyotes...they chased me in the woods,"

Lissy said, confused. "Why would they go after Shadow Chaser instead of me?"

"Hmmm," Twiggedy snickered, "I think maybe Coyote had a bone to pick with Shadow Chaser—or perhaps a porcupine quill or two!"

They had a good laugh and Lissy hugged each of them. Then Twiggedy wiped her eyes and said, "Girls, I think it's about time for us to go home—all of us."

CHAPTER TWENTY-THREE –
Going Home

The sun was high in the sky as the four headed toward
the shore to fetch the canoe. Waves rocked the little boat
as Lissy reached for the paddle. She was bending over
to push it out of the rocks when she felt for the crystal
necklace about her neck.

"My necklace, it's gone!" Lissy quickly looked around
for her shadow. She clutched at her throat frantically.

"Don't worry, it's still there, you just can't see it,"
Rose said, her brown eyes squinting as she looked across
the lake. Lissy put a hand to her throat again. This time
she felt the glowing warmth of the invisible crystal's
energy. She looked at Rose to ask her about the necklace,
but then followed the woman's gaze over the water. Rose
wasn't looking toward her home on Beaver Isle, but

somewhere nearby. Lissy squinted her eyes, too, and shaded them with her hand. There, on the far side of the lake, was a hill and a cabin and a gray, weathered dock.

"Well, we must be getting home now," sighed Twiggedy casually, as if she had a million things to tend to. But Lissy didn't hear her—she had already gotten into the canoe and paddled across the lake toward the dock jutting out from the maple-dotted shore.

As she neared the opposite shore, she paddled through the shallows, the waves lapping musically against the sandy beach. She steadied herself and got out of the canoe, leaving it bobbing in the water near the dock. She paused to look up at the tall maple tree standing guard.

She climbed the wooden steps leading up the steep hill of pines. At the top, sunshine danced through the trees, leaving golden puddles of light on the soft, needle-covered ground. The towering evergreens sang, whispering softly in her ears. Lissy's heart stopped for a moment as she looked upon the cabin where the whole adventure had begun.

The crisp air seemed to promise snow as it bit at Lissy's nose. She listened to the trees dropping the last of their leaves. Indian Summer would soon be over, Lissy caught herself thinking. Then she whirled around in wonder. It was if she had never left. But she had. She did. Yet....

Tears streaming down her cheeks, she felt her stomach tighten. She ran to the door, swung it open and stepped inside. The cabin's familiar odor of coffee and wool blankets was like perfume, and the little red-checkered curtains waved in the breeze as if to welcome her.

Her eyes fell on the sunlit table. Lissy held her breath and slowly walked over to it. There was her "good book," the Child's Garden of Verses. A breeze lifted the corner of the worn yellow page as golden light played upon her favorite verse. Lissy read it aloud:

"When children are playing alone on the green, in comes the playmate that was never seen. When children are happy and lonely and good, the Friend of children comes out of the wood."

She closed her tear-filled eyes and the soft, tattered book. Holding it tightly to her chest, she wished as hard as she could this happiness would never go away.

"Elizabeth!" she heard a voice call from outside. She jumped, then smiled at the sound of her name and ran to the door. Standing in the dappled sunlight near the car were her mother, father and Bob.

"Come on, dear, get your book. We'll be late," her mother said, smiling at her. Lissy was so confused she didn't know what to say. She felt as if she were in a dream. A good dream.

"I-I want to say goodbye to the lake, Mother," she said, feeling a little dizzy.

Bob came running up to her, "I'll race ya to the dock!"

Lissy whirled around in disbelief. She looked at her mother, "Go ahead and say goodbye, honey. Hand me your book and I'll pack it for you."

Lissy's light-headed feeling vanished as she hopped down each step to the bottom. Bob was standing at the top step, his blond hair blowing in the wind.

"Aw, you beat me, sis," he said, flashing a wide grin. She walked to the shore and looked out over the lake. A tall heron stood eyeing her from the shallows. It squawked at the sight of the children and flew off, its long, graceful wings barely skimming the surface of the water.

"Twiggedy? Rose? Gerty?" Lissy whispered, choking back tears. She heard the knocking of a woodpecker up high in the maple. She followed the sound up the trunk and spotted the bird through the tree canopy. It darted past Lissy and dropped something at her feet. She looked down and lying in the grass was a small, red, plastic canoe with a chip in its side.

"Thank you," she whispered to her friends as she picked it up. Bob came running over to see what she had. At first she held it tightly, but then she opened her fingers and showed him her treasure.

"Well, what do ya know?" he whistled, looking at the toy. "That'll make a neat good luck charm, sis."

"Yeah, it will," Lissy smiled, slipping it into her pocket. They heard their mother call and they ran up the steps to the waiting car. Mother looked beautiful and regal in her pale, green suit and a silver necklace with a crystal teardrop. Lissy felt her heart melt and ran to her mother, hugging her tightly.

"Well, Elizabeth Ann, whatever has gotten into you?" her mother said laughing, stroking Lissy's chestnut-brown hair. Lissy turned to look up at her mother as if to say something, but then couldn't think what it could be. She took one more look back toward the little cabin.

High above the moss-covered roof a small, gray owl was perched in a pine tree. It turned to face Lissy and winked one golden eye at her.

Lissy smiled at the bird as she got into the car, and this time she made sure that the door was shut tightly.

To

The Magical Child

There are windows that appear throughout the day,
    That beckon the brave to come out to play—
      They appear in that certain slant of light,
      Of voiceless morning or dark of night—
    When beyond the silence a ringing is heard
Now's the time to jump! To leap up like a bird
Through the dreaming door which cannot be seen,
Somewhere in the middle of betwixt 'n' between—
There are those who will heed adventure's call,
And those that choose not to journey forth at all—
    For a moment they will go, for a life-
      time they shall stay
    And when they come back, life
      will no longer be gray—
For they have ventured into that enchanted space,
    And have heard the bright laughter of
      The Wild Magic place.

Twiggedy-Jig

North Woods

Cedar Lake

Pine Rock Island

Beaver Isle

Popple-Pine Forest